**He placed his palm** ~~she was encased in the dress, his touch~~ **seemed to penetrate the fabric, as if her skin was laid bare to his caress.**

"There won't be any shortcuts with me and you. I want to get to know you, and I want to take my time doing it." He leaned low, his face mere inches from hers. "No shortcuts."

"Mmm." It was the only sound she could manage. She looked into his hazel eyes and felt her insides melt.

Hooking his finger beneath her chin, he whispered, "Can I?"

She didn't need an explanation to know what he was asking. "Please do."

She saw him smile as he tilted her face to an angle more to his liking. Seconds later, his lips touched hers, and her eyes closed as the sweetness spread through her like wildfire. His lips were soft, and she relished the feeling of them. None of her fantasies had matched this sweet, fiery reality. He kissed her solidly, yet gently, lingering for a few long moments before easing away.

Dear Reader,

Thank you for picking up a copy of *A Love Like This*. I'm so glad you decided to join me as I embark on this new series, and I hope you'll enjoy it. The creative process can be a funny thing, and I had to do a lot of untangling to reach the final product, but the results were totally worth it.

When I was creating the island of Sapphire Shores, I took inspiration from the region of North Carolina known as the Crystal Coast, and the barrier islands. Places like Wrightsville Beach (where I often retreat for vacation or to catch up on writing), Atlantic Beach and Ocracoke Island inspired the beautiful scenery you're about to explore. Devon and Hadley's romance is the perfect start to this series, and I hope you'll love their story as much as I enjoyed writing it.

I love hearing from readers, so feel free to let me know what you think. Reach out to me on Twitter, @KiannaWrites, or Facebook.com/kiannawrites.

All the best,

*Kianna*

# A LOVE LIKE THIS

## Kianna Alexander

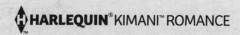
HARLEQUIN® KIMANI™ ROMANCE

Recycling programs
for this product may
not exist in your area.

ISBN-13: 978-0-373-86526-0

A Love Like This

For questions and comments about the quality of this book please contact us
at CustomerService@Harlequin.com.

Printed in U.S.A.

**Kianna Alexander**, like any good Southern belle, wears many hats: loving wife, doting mama, advice-dispensing sister and gabbing girlfriend. She's a voracious reader, an amateur seamstress and occasional painter in oils. Chocolate, American history, sweet tea and Idris Elba are a few of her favorite things. A native of the Tar Heel state, Kianna still lives there with her husband, two kids and a collection of well-loved vintage '80s Barbie dolls. You can keep up with Kianna's releases and appearances by signing up for her mailing list at www.authorkiannaalexander.com/sign-up.

### Books by Kianna Alexander

### Harlequin Kimani Romance

*This Tender Melody*
*Every Beat of My Heart*
*A Sultry Love Song*
*Tempo of Love*
*A Love Like This*

In memory of Rev. Dr. L. E. Davis. My pastor through childhood, he performed my marriage and became my friend in adulthood. Your smile is lighting up heaven now, Rev.

## Acknowledgments

To my Destin Divas, you have been my rock and my support through it all as I travel this sometimes bumpy road. Your love, wisdom and kindness are a balm to my soul. Thank you all for being the queens you are.

To Jennifer and the ladies of the Royal Kourt, thank you for your efforts. You rock!

To my readers, thank you so much for your support. Some of you have been with me since the beginning and some of you are new, but you are all special to me.

To my sister, Erica, I may not say so, but your praise of my writing and my mothering means a lot to me. I love you, Crazy.

To my children, I love you so much. Mommy slays these words every day so you can have a good life.

And to my husband, Keith, you are the best and brightest thing in my life. I couldn't do what I do without you, not just because of your unwavering support, but because you show me just how deep love can be every single day. I love you endlessly.

# Chapter 1

Hadley Monroc leaned against the window seat in the living room of rental unit seven, a clipboard in hand. Her eyes swept the room as she took in the flurry of activity going on around her. As office manager and resident jill-of-all-trades at her family's real estate company, Monroe Holdings, she often oversaw the preparation of a vacation property for a client. Today, however, was a bit different.

She glanced over her shoulder briefly, taking in the scenery outside. The bright sunlight streaming through the sheer white curtains gave no clue to the mid-December chill hanging in the air. Less than a half mile from the grassy lawn fronting the two-story town house the frothy waves of the Atlantic lapped at the sandy shore. She smiled as she turned back to the work at hand, reminded once again why she'd chosen to remain in Sapphire Shores after graduation. Her small island hometown just off the coast of North Carolina possessed gorgeous scenery and a close-knit community she doubted she'd find elsewhere.

Stifling a yawn, Hadley shifted her weight and scanned the room for the familiar face of her friend.

Belinda Quick, owner of Quick Transformations, rushed around the room with a clipboard of her own. Dressed in a pair of blue jeans and a red T-shirt emblazoned with her logo, she stood out among the purple T-shirts worn by her employees. It was Belinda's staff that tackled the responsibility of readying MHI's rental properties between clients. Belinda's business handled a bevy of tasks, from general cleaning to decorating, and their efficiency had proven a godsend for Hadley on more than one occasion. Having known Belinda since high school, Hadley placed the utmost trust in her.

Her sneakers squeaking against the recently polished hardwood floor, Belinda sidled up to Hadley. "What do you think? Are we almost there?"

Hadley drew a deep breath as she looked around again, taking in the meticulously placed Christmas decorations put up by Belinda and her staff. The seven-foot Fraser fir occupying the corner by the staircase leading to the second floor was festooned in red and gold ornaments. The color scheme carried through to the tree skirt, the tablecloth and place mats on the dining room table, and the red and gold velvet bows adorning the balsam garland fastened to the fireplace mantel. "It looks fantastic, B. You've done it again, girl."

Belinda winked. "You know QT never slacks on a job. Got a few lights strung outside, too."

Hadley's brow wrinkled. "You remembered to only use white lights, right? Because…"

"I know, I know. Mr. Granger doesn't like colored lights." Belinda rolled her eyes playfully. "It's all good, girl. We only used white lights. On the tree, outside, the whole nine. And no decor on the second floor, just like you asked."

Hadley felt a shiver go down her spine, and it wasn't due to lack of insulation in the rental unit, either. It was the shiver that always moved through her when anyone mentioned Devon Granger's name. *Devon Granger.* Her tongue darted out to moisten her bottom lip as she thought of him. That man had a body so solid and a face so handsome, it was if he'd been hewn from a block of marble. She was sure she wasn't the only woman who found the actor, famous for his performances in action films and Westerns, irresistibly sexy. She was, however, the only woman who'd spent the last four Christmases making sure his every need was met to his satisfaction. Well, his rental property needs, anyhow. Given the chance, though, Hadley knew she'd happily fulfill just about any request he could throw her way…

"Hadley. Hadley!" Belinda snapped her fingers several times. "Are you still with me, girl?"

Blinking a few times until her friend's face came into focus, Hadley smiled sheepishly. "Sorry, B. What did you say?"

"I said, I'm telling my staff to clear out so you and I can make our final walk-through."

"Great. I think we're done here. He likes his decorations to be pretty low-key." Hadley hoped if she steered the conversation right back to the business at hand, her friend wouldn't call her out for daydreaming. *Honestly, it's her fault for bringing up his name.*

No such luck. Belinda's brow hitched upward, as it was apt to do before she commenced grilling someone for information. "You were fantasizing about him again, weren't you." It was a question, yet she posed it as a statement, as if there weren't any doubt in her mind about the answer.

Hadley sucked in a breath. *Oh, the things I could tell her.* She knew there was no point in trying to conceal her plans from Belinda, but that didn't mean she wanted all eight of her friend's employees to know her personal business. "Go clear out the staff, B."

She shrugged. "Fair enough. But once they leave, I want the dirt, Hadley."

Shaking her head, Hadley watched her friend walk away and begin the process of rounding up her employees. She plopped down on the cushion of the window seat, waiting until the last of the staff members had left and watched as Belinda strode back over.

"Let's get this walk-through knocked out." Belinda gestured for Hadley to get up. "And while we do it, you can tell me what you're plotting."

Hadley shook her head as the two of them began walking the property. "You know me too well."

"Yep. So you may as well let the tiger out of the sack."

Hadley sighed. "Well, you know I've had a thing

for Devon ever since he first rented from us several years ago."

Belinda scoffed. "A thing for him? Girl, please. You've been pining after that man like you're a woman in a desert and he's the oasis."

She pursed her lips. "Thanks for that colorful description, B. Anyway, I've stayed away from him because I knew he was grieving, and I respected that. But I think five years is more than reasonable, don't you?" Around town, it was common knowledge that escaping to the vacation house had been part of Devon's way of coping with the loss of his wife. Regardless of her strong feelings for him, Hadley could never bring herself to infringe on his grief.

Belinda nodded as they rounded the corner, passing the tree to head upstairs. "Yes, Hadley. Five years is very respectable. You've been very patient, considering how obsessed you are with him."

On the landing, Hadley gave Belinda a playful punch on the shoulder. "Shut up, B. It's not an obsession. It's not like I have an altar to him or something."

A chuckling Belinda cracked open the door to the master bedroom. "You know I'm just playing with you. But you have to admit, you've got it pretty bad."

Hadley could feel her face relaxing, and she could see her softening expression reflected at her in the bedroom mirror. "Yeah, you're right. And this year, I'm going to do something about it. It's my Christmas gift to myself."

She looked around the space. Belinda's crew had done a great job, and she admired the freshly made four-poster, king-size bed. The bed, along with the matching nightstands and dresser, were all fashioned of polished oak and adorned with an etched ivy-leaf pattern. The soft grey carpet felt like a cloud beneath her feet.

They left the bedroom and continued through the upper floor.

"More power to you. Get your man, girl." Belinda peeked into the bathroom. "Do you have a plan for how you're going to approach him?"

Hadley answered as they finished checking the upstairs room and descended the stairs. "I've got a start. I'm going to meet him at arrival and give him a gift to thank him for renting from us for the past five years. That will get me in, at least." It was something the company did all the time for repeat clients, and making the delivery herself gave her a perfect excuse to spend time in Devon's company.

Back in the living room, Belinda turned to Hadley and tossed her the keys. "That will get you in, true enough. But once you're alone, what are you going to say to him?"

Hadley imagined his face and shook her head. "I don't have the faintest idea. I guess I'm winging it." After all these years of denying herself this particular piece of dark chocolate, she just hoped she'd be coherent enough to get her point across.

The two women left the unit laughing, and Hadley locked the door behind them.

Devon Granger moved around the master bedroom of his Los Angeles home, tossing things into the open suitcase lying on his bed. His flight to North Carolina would depart in a few hours, and he needed to get it together if he expected to make it in time to board the plane. Flying out of LAX was one of his least favorite things to do—the place never seemed to have a time when it wasn't crowded. Still, it was the closest airport to his Silver Lake home. Going a little early meant he wouldn't have to rush.

Devon's work as an actor had left him more than financially secure, but he wasn't the type of guy to spend his money on private jets, yachts and other things he saw as unnecessary. He just flew first or business class, concealed his identity, and kept to himself on flights and in airports. Other than the occasional overzealous fan who'd demand an autograph or selfie, his system had served him well over the years.

He stopped to regard the suitcase, his eyes scanning the contents. He'd packed mainly comfortable clothing for his annual holiday vacation, and he looked forward to lounging around his favorite beach rental overlooking the Atlantic. Force of habit made him also pack slacks, button-downs and a few ties, just in case.

As he leaned over the bed to tuck his socks into an outer compartment, a twinge shot through his lower back. Grimacing, he jerked upright again before uttering a low curse. He was still relatively young, just shy of thirty-five. Despite his youth, his recent injury had made him question whether he should keep performing his own stunts in his action roles.

Before Thanksgiving, he'd shot the final scene for the upcoming *Destruction Derby 3*. When he'd made the daring leap, escaping an explosion that would be added in later via the magic of special effects, he'd landed improperly, resulting in a herniated disk. It wasn't the first time he'd been injured while executing a stunt, but it was his most serious injury to date.

The bed began buzzing, drawing his attention back to the moment at hand. He searched around until he located his phone, tucked between the suitcase and his comforter. Grabbing it, he answered the call on speaker. "Hi, Ma. How are you?"

Eva Sykes Granger's voice filled the room. "I'm fine, but how are you? Is your back okay?"

"It's fine, Ma." It wasn't a lie, per se. Once he took his medication and gave it time to get into his system, he'd be feeling somewhat better.

"Are you sure you're up to that long flight? Don't you think you should sit out the vacation this year?" Her words were laced with motherly concern.

"I wouldn't think of it." He'd come to look forward to this getaway, far from the fast-paced hustle and bustle of LA. He craved the respite of the quiet oceanfront hamlet where he'd been born. "Besides, it's not a nonstop flight. I've got a layover in Dallas, and I'll be sure to stretch."

She sighed. "Well, you're an adult. I don't suppose I can stop you from going."

He shook his head, tucking his last item of clothing into the suitcase and closing it. "Ma, you know why I go home every year. What I don't know is why you and Dad don't come with me. You know I'd cover your tickets."

Another sigh. "Christmas in North Carolina is a bit

much for your father and me. You know we aren't religious, and we're happier keeping things low-key this time of year."

He chuckled. "I know, Ma. You and Dad aren't exactly filled with the Christmas spirit." His parents lived in a palatial home he'd bought them when he had completed his first film, but David and Eva's idea of holiday decoration consisted of battery-operated candles in the front windows and a single strand of white lights, placed in a palm tree by their gardener.

As if reading his mind, she said, "I know what you're thinking, Devon. And I'll have you know Mr. Roper strung lights in *two* of our palm trees this year."

Grateful his mother couldn't see him rolling his eyes, he quipped, "Don't overdo it now, Ma."

She laughed, the familiar sound warming Devon's heart. "Oh, go on with you. Make sure you call us and let us know you got there safely."

"I always do." He zipped the suitcase closed, placing his trusty lock in the loops to secure it.

"Devon...there's one more thing."

Noticing the hesitation in her tone, he sat down on the edge of the bed. "What is it, Ma?"

"Your father and I were talking, and we really want to see you settled down again."

He sighed. He'd been hoping to avoid this conversation this year, but it seemed that wasn't going to happen. "Ma. I don't really want to talk about this."

"I know you don't, son, so just hear me out. It's been five years since Nat left us, and we're ready for you to get off the merry-go-round and find a nice girl to bring home."

"Merry-go-round? Really, Ma?" He'd started dating again about two years ago, and since then he'd gone out with his share of women. He'd even satisfied his urges here and there, but the term his mother had just used seemed to go too far in describing his life as a young widower.

"You've dated plenty of girls but never gotten serious about anyone. I know it must be hard to put your heart on the line after such a loss, but you've got to take the chance, dear."

He felt his brow furrow. *Hard* didn't begin to describe it. His reluctance to enter a serious relationship again had nothing to do with opportunity and everything to do with his feelings. His wife, Natalie, had been only twenty-nine when he'd lost her to an undetected congenital heart defect. It had taken him almost three years to learn to navigate the world without his childhood sweetheart by his side.

"Just think about it, dear. That's all we ask."

He could hear the love and concern in his mother's voice, and it did much to soothe his frustration. "I will, Ma." And he would think about it. But that didn't guarantee he'd come home with a fiancée any time soon, and he hoped she realized that. "I love you."

"I love you, too, son. Travel safe." She disconnected the call.

Devon stood and pocketed his phone, glancing around his room to be sure he hadn't forgotten anything he'd need for his trip. That done, he dropped the wheeled suitcase on the floor, lifted the telescoping handle and pushed it out of the room.

## Chapter 2

Hadley pulled her midnight blue sedan up to the curb in front of the rental unit and cut the engine. Unbuckling her seat belt, she dropped the driver-side visor and opened the lighted vanity mirror. She took a moment to make sure her upswept hair and carefully applied makeup were on point, then righted the visor and smiled.

Devon was due to arrive any minute now. She'd always known him to be punctual, and that was just one of the qualities he possessed that made him so attractive. She knew she wouldn't have to wait long for him to appear, so she gathered her wits.

She still didn't know what she would say to him, other than the rote script she always gave to longtime customers when she delivered their appreciation gifts.

She'd thank him for his loyalty, just as her brothers would expect. That would be the easy part. What came after that, she had no idea. There was no point in trying to plan what to say to him now. She fully expected that when she looked into his gorgeous golden eyes, she wouldn't remember her name, let alone any impassioned speech she planned to make.

She looked down at her outfit. She'd chosen a close-fitting sweater, slim jeans and knee-high boots. Her aim was to be appealing to Devon's eyes while still looking professional. She'd also considered the conditions outside. Despite the bright sunshine, the temperature hovered somewhere in the low fifties. She possessed more enticing outfits, but she was looking to make a certain impression. Besides, no one looked sexy while shivering.

The sound of an approaching engine drew her attention, and she checked her rearview. Seeing Devon approaching in a midsize SUV made her lips stretch into a smile. This was another thing she liked about him. Here he was, rich and famous for his acting, yet he eschewed the bodyguards, drivers and entourage many people in his position had. She had no idea how he lived his life in LA, but it was clear that he didn't make himself fodder for the celebrity-gossip bloggers and television shows. And when he was home in Sapphire Shores, he was about as low-key as a person could get. He flew commercial, rented a car and drove himself where he needed to go.

She sighed as she watched him navigate the vehicle into the driveway. *He's so down-to-earth.*

Gathering the large gift basket she'd brought with her from the office onto her lap, she slipped out of the car as gracefully as she could. Once she'd closed her door, she stood by her car, watching and waiting. She tamped down her excitement at seeing him again, not wanting to ambush him before he had a chance to get out of his car.

His driver's side door swung open then, and as he stepped out and stood to his full height, Hadley could feel her heartbeat racing. Dark sunglasses obscured his eyes, but nothing obstructed her view of the rest of his smooth, brown-skinned face. She reveled in the sight of his thick dark brows, his perfectly groomed mustache and beard, and the full, soft-looking lips centering it all. His long, lean body was dressed casually in a pair of khakis, a green sweater and brown loafers. The clothes weren't tight, but they were fitted enough that she could see the hard lines of his muscles flexing beneath the fabric as he moved.

To Hadley's appreciative eyes, he almost seemed to be moving in slow motion. Her lips parted, allowing a pent-up breath to escape into the cool winter air. She tightened her arms around the gift basket, knowing that if she didn't, it might fall to the ground, forgotten, as she stared at her favorite client. *How can he be that damn fine?*

He opened the hatch at the back of the vehicle. Dragging out a wheeled suitcase, he shut the hatch again and turned her way. "Hadley, is that you?"

She shifted the basket, offering a wave before shifting it back into both hands. "It's me," she called. "How are you?" As she spoke, she started walking in his direction.

"I'm good, thanks. How about you?" He remained by the back of the SUV, as if waiting for her.

A few more long steps brought her into his personal space. "Good, good. Can't complain."

He smiled, showing off two rows of shimmering white teeth. "Glad to hear it."

That familiar tingle started at the back of her neck, and she did her best to ignore it. Extending the basket in his direction, she spoke. "This is for you, from all of us at Monroe Holdings. We want to thank you for your loyalty in renting from us for five consecutive years."

"Thank you, Hadley. That's very nice." He extended an arm, taking the basket she'd needed two hands to carry and sweeping it into his grasp as if it weighed nothing. Regarding the selection of fruit, nuts and candy, he looked her way. "Looks like there's some pretty good stuff in here."

She offered a soft smile. "I... I mean, we hope you'll enjoy it." She reached into the hip pocket of her jeans and fished out the key to the unit. "I'll go ahead and let you in so you can put your things down." She started walking toward the front door.

He started to follow, but when he turned, he winced.

The basket slipped from his arms.

Hadley took a wide step and reached out, catching hold of the free end of the shrink-wrap just before the basket could hit the ground. The bottom of it scraped the driveway, but as she raised it to inspect, she found all the contents intact.

He reached up, slipping off his shades and tucking them into the neckline of his sweater.

The moment his intense hazel eyes met hers, Hadley felt a tingle shoot down her spine until it touched the base, then flare out to the rest of her body.

"Wow, Hadley. You've got amazing reflexes." He looked genuinely impressed.

She shrugged, straightening up with the basket in her arms. "I take a kickboxing class." She looked back at him, letting her concern show through. "Are you okay?"

He waved her off. "I'm fine. Just a little twinge in my back that pops up now and again."

She nodded. Even though she suspected there was more to it than he let on, she knew it wasn't her place to press him.

Firmly grasping the handle of his bag, he rolled it to the front door.

As he passed by, she caught a glimpse of his firm backside. It was all she could do to hold onto the basket as she trailed behind him. They walked up the two stone steps to the door. Shifting a bit, she used the key to unlock the place and followed him inside.

He rolled his bag into the nook by the window seat, then glanced around the room. "The decorations are really nice this year. Subtle, but still festive."

She grinned, probably a little wider than she had intended. "That's the look we were going for. I'm glad you like them." She crossed the room to the low mahogany coffee table, setting the gift basket down before any more mishaps could occur.

As she bent, she had the distinct sense that he was

looking at her backside. Acting with intention, she drew
out the motion, staying in the position a few seconds
longer than necessary as she pretended to fuss with the
bow on the basket. When she stood and slowly turned
Devon's way, he was sitting on the cushioned window
seat.

His hazel eyes were focused squarely on her.

When Devon saw Hadley turn around and look at
him, he didn't bother to shift his gaze. He'd misjudged a
few things in his day, but there was no mistaking Hadley's flirting. The exaggerated way she'd bent over the
table just now had obviously been done for his benefit,
and benefit he did. The sight of her round, upturned
ass had warmed his blood so much he was tempted to
strip off his sweater.

As she caught his eye, her full lips curved into a
smile. "Devon. Were you doing what I think you were
doing just now?" The teasing in her tone indicated how
certain she felt of the answer.

He chuckled. "Only if you were doing what I think
you were."

She winked but admitted nothing.

The grin stretching his lips held a mixture of amuse-
ment and intrigue. Since when had Hadley been check-
ing for him? He'd always thought of her as attractive.
But he'd tried not to dwell on that, since there were two
glaring factors that might make her an unsuitable match.
She was only twenty-eight, six years younger than him.
Not to mention she was the baby sister of his old friend
Campbell. He and Campbell had hung out a lot in high

school, and Devon had no idea how Campbell would react to his old cutup buddy going after his sister.

She let her gaze drop in a coy manner.

He kept his expression even, hoping not to sway her one way or the other. He was supposed to be resting over the holidays, not entertaining a tender young thing like Hadley Monroe. Still, the man in him couldn't help but be flattered by her theatrics.

Her expression changed then, indicating a return to her usual all-business demeanor. She sat on the sofa, shifting to face his way. "So, tell me all the interesting things happening on the left coast."

He chuckled. "I was about to ask you for an update on what's been going on here over the past year."

"Not much." She shrugged. "We've cleared our last thirty acres of land and are trying to decide what to develop there. A new grocery store opened, along with a few boutiques to appeal to the tourist crowd."

"What about Coastal High? Did they ever finish the new stadium?" When he'd visited last year, ground had been broken for the project, adjacent to the old field.

"Yes. They finished it right after school let out for the summer. By the time the kids got back for the new school year, the football team had already practiced on the new turf."

He nodded, pleased that his alma mater was making improvements. "You know, I haven't been back to Coastal since I graduated." He watched her as she spoke, taking note of her body language. "It's been so long, I don't think I remember how to get there." He had a vague idea of the way to the school and could probably find it on his own. But he wanted to see how she'd respond.

She leaned forward, her face brightening. "If you want to see the new stadium, I'll take you over there."

"Sounds great. Maybe we'll swing by there in a few days." He wondered if he was encouraging her too much, but he did consider her a friend. He saw no reason he couldn't treat her as such. If she were someone else, someone closer to his age and not related to one of his oldest friends, they'd be having a much different conversation right now.

"Really, though. Tell me what's happening in Hollywood. Filming anything? Premieres coming up?" The glint in her eyes gave away her excitement.

He chuckled at her effortless transition from friend to fan. "I wrapped *Destruction Derby 3* about a month ago. Haven't filmed anything since, and no premieres until after the New Year."

She clapped her hands together. "I can't wait for *DD3* to come out. I loved the first two."

His brow hitched. "Really? I never pegged you for the type who'd like the DD series. Explosions, fast cars, fistfights." The films in the series were wildly popular with the young male audience, at least according to the suits at the studio. They were huge moneymakers and kept Devon financially secure, but filming them had been especially hard on his body.

She made a face of mock offense. "That's sexist. Just because I'm a woman, you think I can't get into a good action thriller?"

"You gotta admit, you're not exactly the target audience."

She rolled her eyes, but her smile remained. "Come on, Devon. You know me better than that."

He laughed. "I'm just teasing you. Thanks for the compliment, though."

She leaned in, dropped her voice as if there were someone else in the room. "Listen, just between me and you, is Captain Vicious coming back for the third movie?"

He laughed again at her question. "You're like the fiftieth person to ask me that." The character, a villain in the DD series, was played by veteran actor Rick Rollingsworth. Rick, a contemporary of Samuel L. and Denzel, was about as well loved as a man of color in Hollywood could expect to be. "At least ten people asked me that between the baggage claim and the rental car counter."

"We're friends, though. So, are you gonna tell me?"

He shook his head. "Sorry. The nondisclosure agreement in my contract is in full effect." He knew Captain Vicious would indeed be making a return but couldn't risk his standing with the studio by telling her that. "You'll have to find out with everybody else when the movie drops in May."

She sighed. "Oh, well. I've waited this long, I suppose I can wait till Memorial Day." She stood and he took time to appreciate his view of her. The sweater, jeans and tall boots encased her shapely figure in a way he found very attractive, but not overly revealing. The dark ringlets of her hair were pinned on top of her head, revealing the lines of her face. Her high cheekbones, full lips and sparkling brown eyes were all marks of her beauty, and of the Monroe blood flowing through her veins. Today, Hadley looked much as her mother, Viola, had looked twenty years ago, when they were kids.

A few long, silent moments passed between them before she seemed to notice his scrutiny. Her cheeks filled with a rosy blush, the glittering eyes shifting to the window behind him. Straightening, she began to run through the speech she usually gave him when he checked in to the unit. "The groceries you requested for the first week are already in the kitchen. You have plenty of fresh linen in the closet upstairs, and the housekeeping service will stop by every other day to do laundry and dishes for you…"

He smiled, putting up his hand to stop her rambling. "Thanks, Hadley. I got it."

She shifted her gaze away from his face, running her hand over the red ribbon securing the gift basket. "Is there anything else you'll need?"

He fought the urge to give her one of the many cheeky answers that came to mind. Shaking his head, he said, "No, but if I think of something I'll give the office a call."

She crossed the room toward the front door, passing him as she moved. "Well, I'll stop pestering you and let you get on with your vacation. Just give the office a call if you need anything, or when you're ready to go see the new stadium."

He nodded. "I will. Thanks for everything, Hadley." His words were sincere. She'd seen to his every need for the past four years he'd been coming there, either personally or through the staff. She made it easy for him to leave his work behind for three glorious weeks, and he truly did appreciate everything she did.

"You're welcome." She smiled on the heels of her soft reply, then opened the door and let herself out.

He turned and looked out the window, watching her stroll back to her car.

Something told him this Christmas would be an interesting one.

# Chapter 3

Seated behind her desk, Hadley popped a soft peppermint in her mouth and chewed. The desktop was full of paperwork, detailing the long list of repairs waiting to be made at several of Monroe's properties. She sighed as she swallowed the small pieces of candy. She was the office manager, and that entailed a lot of things. What it didn't entail was property management—that was Campbell's job.

Scooting her chair back, she stood and walked around her desk. Leaving her office, she walked down the corridor to Savion's office. The door was open, and a quick peek let her see her brother poring over something on his desk. She tapped on the glass panel next to the door to get his attention.

Glancing up, he waved her in. "What's up, Hadley?"

She entered the office and took a seat in one of his guest chairs. The office, which had been occupied by their father, Carver, before his retirement, still looked much the same as it had ten years ago. Savion had held on to most of their father's books and decor, as well as the navy blue carpet and soft-textured blue wallpaper.

Aware of her eldest brother's obsession with detail, she waited silently for a few moments while he finished reading whatever currently had his attention.

He looked up again, closing his magazine and making eye contact with her. "What do you need, sis?"

Seeing that his body language invited conversation, she sat back in her chair. "I've got a pile of repair request forms on my desk. Again."

"That's Campbell's responsibility, not yours."

She pursed her lips. "I know that, Savion. What I want to know is who keeps dropping the forms on my desk instead of handing them over to Cam."

Savion's exaggerated shrug said all. "Must be somebody on staff. Maybe Belinda? Even though she doesn't work for us, she's in and out of here all the time."

She shook her head. "Belinda knows better."

"I don't know. Maybe it's one of her people. Either way, it's Campbell's job to handle that stuff, so just pass the stack to him." He reached up, stifling a yawn with his hand.

She rolled her eyes. Whoever was leaving her brother's work on her desk would catch pure hell from her if she ever caught them. Pushing that aside for now, she spoke again. "Listen. While I'm in here, what's going on with the shoot for the new TV commercial?"

He opened the cover of the black leather-bound planner he kept with him at all times, dropping it on his desk. His eyes were on the pages as he answered her question. "We're supposed to shoot next Wednesday and into Thursday, if necessary. We hope to get it on the air right after the New Year."

"Does it have a script? Are we doing voice-over? Who's going to be in it?"

He looked up, his brow knitting as if he were confused. "Yes, yes and I'm going to be in it. Why are you asking all these questions about the commercial, anyway?"

She shifted in her seat, pushing away her discomfort with his scrutiny. "I have some ideas for the commercial. You know, to punch it up a bit."

Now he looked annoyed. "What's wrong with the commercials we've been making, Hadley?"

She cleared her throat. "Nothing, per se. I just think it's time to try a new direction."

"I don't know why you'd say that. Monroe Holdings isn't lacking for business, despite competition from Rent-A-Retreat and Homeshare Plus, so the commercials must be working."

"Sure they are. I'm not saying they aren't effective." She did her best to temper her response, knowing how much her brother enjoyed being the face of MHI, and how much he hated being contradicted. She was sure the commercials worked, to a degree, and especially with the female audience. Savion, just like Campbell and their father, was a handsome man, and possessed enough charisma to sell sand at the beach. Still, she thought a change of pace would be nice. "I just think it would be good to film an updated concept, something new to add to the rotation of ads."

He wore his skepticism like a mask. "Hadley, why rock the boat? People know me as the spokesman for MHI. It's comforting, familiar. And isn't that what we're all about? Providing clients with comfort?"

She sighed. *This conversation isn't going anywhere.* Once again, her brother had dismissed her idea before she'd even had a chance to properly express it. "Never mind, Savion." She rose from the seat, vowing not to waste any more of her time on the matter—at least not today. "I'm going to go deliver the forms to their rightful owner."

Savion nodded, then returned his attention to his planner.

On the heels of his nonverbal dismissal, Hadley left the office, seeking out her other brother. Before she could make it to the end of the hall, Campbell dashed out of his office and jogged past her.

Spinning around, she called after him. "Cam. You have to get this stack of repair requests—"

"Not now, Hadley. I've got a meeting." He kept walking, his long strides taking him out of the corridor and into the main lobby.

She followed him, half tempted to shake her fist. "A meeting or a date?"

He glanced back at her long enough to shoot her a crooked grin. "Don't hate, sis."

She rolled her eyes. "Cam. It's the middle of the day. You have to do some actual work around here."

"I'll get to it later," he called back as he slipped out through the glass doors, letting them swing shut behind him.

Standing in the lobby alone, Hadley propped her fists on her hips, feeling her face crunch into a frown. Her work at MHI had begun to seem like a combination of babysitting and playing secretary, neither of which she'd signed up to do. Her brothers had always been expected to remain in Sapphire Shores and continue the Monroe legacy of controlling most of the rental property on the island. As the baby of the family, and the only girl, she hadn't had those expectations placed on her. Still, she loved her hometown, and loved her family more. When she'd turned down an executive position out of state to work for the family business as office manager, she hadn't considered it a sacrifice. But as time went by, and she put in more and more work only to be dismissed and undervalued by her brothers, she wondered if she'd made the right choice.

With a shake of her head, she returned to her office. The small digital clock on the desk told her it was almost noon, and as she plopped down in her chair, she contemplated what she'd do for lunch. Leaving the office sounded fabulous, so she decided she'd walk a few blocks down to the nearby shopping center to grab something. The walk would likely do her good by helping to clear her mind and giving her time to let her irritation with her brothers dissipate.

She eyed the stack of repair requests still sitting on her desk. Eight of their rental units needed some repair or other, and four of those were currently occupied. As was standard, those units with people staying in them would take priority over vacant ones. She thought about Campbell, and with no idea of where he'd gone or when he'd be back, she picked up the phone to call the plumbers and technicians needed for the occupied units.

Erring on the side of caution helped her cope with situations like this, and as she waited for the plumber to answer her call, she vowed to give Campbell a smack upside his head the next time she saw him.

Devon thumbed through the pages of *Reader's Digest* as he sat in the waiting room of Stinger Urgent Care. He'd only been in town for forty-eight hours, and already the pain from his herniated disk had become worrisome enough to bring him here. This was the last place he'd wanted to spend the first Friday of his winter vacation, but there hadn't been any way to avoid it.

Trying to take his focus off the pain in his back, he half read an article in the magazine. While he read, he shifted his hips in the seat, a vain attempt at getting comfortable. But with the searing pain radiating through his low back, achieving comfort was an impossibility.

"Mr. Granger?" A scrubs-clad nurse appeared in the doorway to his left, her gaze cast down at the clipboard in her hand. "Devon Granger?"

He put the magazine down and stood, approaching the nurse.

As he walked up, she looked up from her clipboard. Her eyes immediately grew five sizes larger. "Oh. My. God. You're *that* Devon Granger?"

Despite his discomfort, he managed a smile. He had

a lot of genuine gratitude for his fans—their support had given him a very good life. "Yes. And you are?"

Blushing, she looked away, seeming to struggle to remember her name. "I'm…uh…Marla. It's so nice to meet you, Mr. Granger. I loved you in *Reach for the Sky*… It's my favorite movie of all time."

"Thank you, Marla. And please, call me Devon."

A giggle he'd expect to hear from a teenager erupted from her lips, and she stifled it. "Oh my goodness. Let me stop holding you up. Follow me to your exam room." She started walking down the narrow corridor leading to the rear of the clinic.

He followed her, still a bit amused by the encounter. A few seconds later, she escorted him into a room complete with the typical doctor's office setup: a counter with a sink, a short wheeled stool, a chrome and plastic chair, and a paper-covered bed.

As he took a seat in the chair, she spent a few moments taking his vital signs. That done, she headed for the door.

"Dr. Stinger will be in to see you soon." Still smiling, she departed, closing the door behind her.

The hard seat and backrest of the chair made him nostalgic for the one in the waiting area; at least it had been padded. The stiff material wasn't helping his pain any, so he got up and moved to the bed, which was set in the upright position.

He was scooting his hips onto the paper-covered surface when the door swung open.

Dr. Steven Stinger, dressed in dark slacks and a white medical coat embroidered with his name, entered the room and closed the door behind him. A Black man in his late forties, Dr. Stinger wore a pair of black-framed glasses perched on the end of his nose, as well as the traditional stethoscope draped over his neck. "Mr. Granger. What brings you here today?" He took a seat on the wheeled stool and looked Devon's way.

Settling back against the bed, he released a breath. "My back. I have a herniated disk, and I can't deal with the pain anymore."

Dr. Stinger slid the clipboard holding what Devon assumed to be his medical chart from beneath his arm and jotted something on it. "Which disk?"

He swiveled to his left, gesturing to his tailbone region. "It's in the sacrum area."

"Oh. That's a particularly uncomfortable spot." He scribbled some more. "How long have you had the injury, and how have you been dealing with the pain so far?"

"It's been about a month. I injured myself doing a stunt on my last film…"

Dr. Stinger's expression changed, becoming less serious. "*Destruction Derby 3*, right?"

"Yes." He supposed he shouldn't be surprised that the doctor would ask, given the immense popularity of the series. Still, he wanted to steer the conversation back to the pain that had brought him to the clinic. "Anyway, I've been treating it with hot and cold therapy and some turmeric capsules my trainer gave me."

Still making notes, Dr. Stinger nodded. "Is there a reason you didn't get a prescription from the doctor who diagnosed you? In most cases like this, a prescription is offered."

Straightening, Devon scratched his chin. "My doctor did offer a prescription, but I wanted to try the natural remedies first. I'm not the biggest fan of pharmaceuticals, so I avoid them when I can."

"I can understand that. A lot of my patients feel the same way." Dr. Stinger set his pen and chart aside. "Let me examine you to get a better idea of how I can help you going forward. How long will you be in town?"

"Until just after the New Year."

Dr. Stinger adjusted the bed until it lay flat, and then instructed Devon to lie down on his stomach.

The doctor left the room and returned with a portable X-ray machine and the nurse. Once the examination was complete, and the nurse and equipment were out of the room, Dr. Stinger readjusted the bed so Devon could sit upright again.

"I'm going to recommend a nonsteroidal anti-inflammatory for you. Considering your attitude toward medication, I'll start you at a low dose." The doctor quickly wrote on his prescription pad. "Also, you'll need to remain active—walking will help keep the joints lubricated and lessen your discomfort. Where are you staying while you're here?"

"I'm in a rental town house on Rising Tide Drive."

Dr. Stinger's brow hitched. "Two story?"

He nodded.

"You'll need to stay off the second floor. Walking will help, but climbing stairs several times a day will put undue stress on your injury. Can you make arrangements to do that?"

"I guess so." He knew that would involve calling MHI and probably interacting with Hadley again.

"You may also need some help around the house. Standing in one spot, such as for cooking or washing dishes, is probably not going to be comfortable. You should consider hiring someone for that kind of thing." Tearing the prescription from his pad, he handed it over.

Devon accepted the prescription, tucking it into the hip pocket of his jeans. "I'll look into it." The housekeeping staff already kept the place clean for him, but he'd still need to make some adjustments. Plus, he'd planned to cook for himself, since he didn't want to spend two and a half weeks eating takeout. Now he'd have to see if Hadley could spare a staff member to be at his disposal.

As Devon left the clinic, heading for the pharmacy two doors down, he inhaled, letting the ocean breeze fill his nostrils. The air in Los Angeles was notoriously dirty, and deep inhales there often involved suffering through some unpleasant odors. Here, all he smelled was the salt, the sand and the grass.

Coming here once a year did him a world of good. It wasn't just about escaping the busyness of life in LA—it was about returning home to the place that had shaped his youth. Doing that gave him a sense of peace, and he'd sorely needed that when he lost Natalie.

As he swung open the door to the pharmacy, he contemplated what he would say to Hadley when he

called the office to make his requests. She'd said to
call if he needed anything, and now he'd have to take
her up on that.

# Chapter 4

Friday afternoon, Hadley was stretched out on the love seat in her office with her head resting on one of the arms. She held her cell phone to her ear, listening to her mother on the other end of the line.

"Hadley, say something, honey. We need to decide what we're serving so I can send out for the groceries." At fifty-six, Viola Monroe was still as fastidious as ever when it came to her holiday menu. While she loved to cook, she hated to shop and always arranged to have the groceries delivered to the house.

"I know, Mama. I like what you've mentioned so far." Hadley tossed one jeans-clad leg over the other, resting her ankles on the opposite arm of the love seat from where she reclined. "We should definitely do a glazed ham. It's tradition, and I don't think anybody wants to change it. And the turkey breast was a big hit with the guys last year."

"We'll keep those things. But we need to decide on some side dishes to go along with them." Viola paused a moment before launching into a list. "We need at least three vegetables, two starches, desserts…"

While her mother went on and on about the menu for Christmas dinner, Hadley found her mind wandering. That was common whenever Viola started obsessing about the minutiae of the holiday meal. Today, however, Hadley's mind wandered into the most enticing territory. She recalled Devon's arrival in town, and the time she'd spent in the town house with him. Her mind replayed the intense look in his hazel eyes, the way he'd smiled at her. She inhaled and could swear she smelled his woodsy, masculine cologne. She imagined what his arms must look like beneath that sweater, what the hard lines of his chest might feel like beneath her palms…

"Hadley, are you listening to me?"

Snapped back to reality by the harsh tone of her mother's voice, she swung her legs down and sat up. "Sorry, Mama. I'm swamped with work around here, so my mind wandered a bit."

"Mmm-hmm." Viola didn't sound convinced in the least. "I said, we'll have roasted potatoes, stuffing, glazed brussels sprouts, green beans and turnip greens to round out the meal."

"Sounds fantastic."

"Then I asked *you* what we should have for dessert."

Frantically searching her mind for an answer, Hadley nervously drummed her fingers on her thigh. Then she remembered a conversation she'd had with Devon the previous year about his favorite desserts. "Why don't we have Dutch apple pie and peach cobbler?"

After a few beats, Viola answered, "I like it. We haven't had those in years, not since your father got on this tiramisu kick."

Hadley breathed a sigh of relief.

"Now that we've settled that, why don't you tell me what you were really thinking about just now when you were ignoring me?"

Her eyes widened as she realized her relief had been premature. "I, uh…well, I found another stack of repair request forms on my desk yesterday, and Cam wouldn't—"

Viola scoffed. "Oh, please. You're my daughter. I've only known you since you took your first breath. And I know good and well you weren't thinking about anything related to work."

Falling back against the cushioned backrest of her love seat, Hadley sighed. "It's nothing. It's just that Devon checked in Wednesday, and I've been a bit… distracted."

Viola's soft chuckle met that admission. "Honey, I know he's here. He's a celebrity. Everybody knows he's here. What I want to know is when are you going to ask him over for Christmas dinner?"

She bristled. "Mama. I've asked him to join us for dinner for the past four years, and every time he's turned me down." Devon had always pointed to his desire to spend the day in reflective solitude. She wasn't sure that was the full story, but who was she to question his choice?

"Maybe the fifth time will be the charm. I respect his wishes if he says no again, but at least ask him, honey. Nobody should be alone on Christmas, and we have so much to share."

As much as she'd love to bring Devon home for Christmas—if only to corner him under some mistletoe—she still doubted he'd be receptive to her invitation. "I don't know, Mama."

Viola cleared her throat. "Hadley Aria Monroe, you are going to ask Devon to join us for Christmas dinner, do you understand?"

"Yes, ma'am." She could tell from her mother's tone that she didn't have a choice.

"Heavens, girl. The worst he can do is say no. It isn't as if he's going to run you over with his car for inviting him." Viola chuckled again. "Okay, I'll let you go. And tell your brothers they'd better straighten up or I'll send your father over there."

That comment brought a giggle out of her. "Thanks, Mama. 'Bye."

After she ended the call with her mother, she rose from the love seat and returned to her desk. While she usually tried to leave early on Friday afternoons, she had a bit more work she wanted to do before she started her weekend. Easing into the seat, she flipped open her laptop.

Before the computer could awaken from sleep mode, her office line rang. Lifting the receiver from the cradle, she placed it to her ear. "Hello?"

"Hi, Hadley. It's Devon."

Her heart leaped into her throat the moment she heard his voice. He didn't need to identify himself; there was no mistaking the sexy baritone she often heard whispering to her in her dreams at night. It took a few seconds to find her voice, and when she did, her words tumbled out in a rush. "Devon, hi. How are you? Is everything okay with your rental unit?"

He chuckled. "Everything's fine, I just need a little bit of help. I knew you were the right person to call."

She smiled, wrapping the spiral telephone cord around her index finger like a love-struck teenager as she replied, "I sure am. What can I do for you?"

"I went to the doctor to have my back checked out, and it turns out I need to avoid going up and down stairs."

Hadley's mind automatically swung into problem-solving mode. Flipping open the property book on her desk, she leafed through the pages. "We could move you, but I don't think we have any single-story units available until after the New Year."

"That's fine. I love this place, and I don't really want to move out of it, anyway."

Her brow creased into a frown. "So, what would you like to do? I certainly don't want you going against the doctor's orders."

"Oh, I won't. I have no desire for my back to get any worse."

"How can I help, then?"

"Could you possibly spare a staff member to come

over here and rearrange things for me so I don't have to use the second floor?"

It was an unexpected request, but it confirmed her suspicions that he hadn't been telling her the full story about his back. She thought about the layout of the unit for a moment. What he'd asked for seemed doable. Since there was a bedroom and a three-piece bath on the first floor, the arrangement would work fine. "Sure, I'll send someone right over. They will be there within the hour, in fact."

"Great." The tone of his voice indicated he was smiling. "Thanks a lot, Hadley. I really appreciate it."

"You know how much we value your business. Don't worry, I'll make sure you're taken care of."

"Perfect. Thanks again." And he disconnected the call.

Unraveling her fingertips from the cord, Hadley sighed. Then she returned the receiver to the cradle and sat back in her chair, grinning. An opportunity had presented itself, and she wasn't about to miss it. She'd promised to send someone over to help him, and she would. She simply hadn't said whom.

*I have the perfect staffer in mind to take care of Devon.*

*Me.*

Devon had just bent to grab a soda from the bottom of the refrigerator when he heard the knock at the door. He shut the fridge, with his ginger ale in hand, and went to answer it. *Hadley wasn't kidding about getting some-*

*one over here quickly.* It had only been about a half hour since he'd put in the call to the office.

He strolled to the door, looking out the bay window as he passed it. Noting the MHI company car sitting in the driveway, he didn't bother to check the peephole before swinging the door open.

He'd expected to find some guy in the all-blue MHI uniform, ready to do his bidding.

Instead, as the door opened, he came face-to-face with Hadley. She stood on the porch, wearing a long-sleeved blue MHI T-shirt, a pair of dark skinny jeans, high-top sneakers and the most alluring smile he'd ever seen.

He'd been hanging around the town house in a loose tank and athletic shorts and suddenly felt very aware of his attire. Apparently, Hadley shared that awareness, because he saw her eyes rake over his body. Then her gaze lifted to meet his.

"Hi, Devon."

His name on her lips sounded almost musical. "Hi, Hadley. I thought you were sending someone over."

She shrugged, as if she did this sort of thing all the time. "Everyone else was either out on a job or had already gone home by the time you called. Don't worry. I'll take care of you." Her lashes fluttered as she gazed up at him.

He sensed the double meaning in her words. He smiled, folding his arms over his chest. "So, you're sure you'll be able to move everything I need to be rearranged?"

She laughed, a tinkling sound reminiscent of ice

cubes falling into a glass. Bending her arms at the elbows in a show of strength, she quipped, "Kickboxing, remember? I got it. Now, are you gonna let me come in?"

Shaking his head, he stepped aside to allow her entry. Once she'd crossed the threshold, he closed the door behind her and locked it.

She strode to the center of the living room, near the coffee table, and turned his way. Cracking her knuckles, she asked, "What do you need me to do, Devon?"

The more he watched her move—and considered the way her petite, shapely figure looked even in casual clothing—the more he thought about asking her to do things that would probably be very bad for his back. Shaking those thoughts away, he gestured to the stairs that led to the second floor. "First, I need all my clothes and toiletries moved from the master upstairs into the downstairs bedroom."

"No problem." She crossed the room and jogged up the stairs.

He watched her go, again appreciating the view of her ample backside as she climbed the steps. He took a deep breath, wondering how he would keep his thoughts on the task at hand and off her body. The attraction crackling between them was palpable, and part of him knew it had been there for at least the past three years. It was possible she'd been attracted to him before that, and that he'd simply been too wrapped up in his grief over losing Natalie to notice.

Now, as the passage of time lightened the burden of the loss, he saw Hadley in a new light. But the fact remained: she was Campbell Monroe's baby sister. Not to mention their oldest sibling, Savion. Since Savion had been two years ahead of Devon and Campbell in school, Devon didn't really know him that well. Still, every interaction he'd ever had with Savion painted him a serious, exacting man who'd likely be content with his baby sister staying single forever.

She returned about fifteen minutes later, descending the stairs with his suitcase in one hand and his toiletry bag in the other. "I went through the closet and the dresser, folded all your stuff and put it in here. Then I cleared everything around the bathroom sink and put it in the toiletry bag." She moved toward him, extending the bags in his direction. "Look through it and make sure I got everything. Then I'll help you set it all up downstairs."

He took his bags to the window seat, where he opened them and inspected the contents as she stood nearby, waiting. "There are only two things missing. My sneakers and my slippers—they're under the bed."

"Got it." She dashed up the stairs again, returning with the shoes. "Is that everything?"

He nodded, impressed with her eagerness to help. "Yes, thank you."

She smiled again, the corners of her glossy pink lips upturned. "I was just thinking, you'll need the linens from the closet upstairs, too. Why don't you go ahead and start putting your things in the downstairs bedroom, and I'll move the linens to the downstairs closet?"

"Sounds good." He watched her walk away again, then took his bags into the downstairs bedroom. The room was well appointed, though not as much as the master upstairs. The decor was all done in varying shades of blue, from the dark carpet to the textured medium-blue wallpaper and the softer blues echoed in the bedding. It would meet his needs nicely. The only downfall was the queen-size bed. He preferred the king upstairs, due to his height. But for the sake of his back, he would manage fine with the queen.

He went around the room, putting away his clothes again, the same way he had on the day he'd arrived. Once he'd done that and slid his empty suitcase into the closet, he grabbed his toiletry bag from the bed and headed for the bathroom.

He moved into the bathroom, which was much smaller than the one upstairs, and swung open the mirrored medicine cabinet to put away his stuff. The pedestal sink left him no space to leave toothpaste and whatnot around it, so he tucked away everything he'd need daily and shut the cabinet. He looked to the shower stall, glad the downstairs bathroom had one so he wouldn't have to climb the stairs to bathe. Satisfied, he tucked the empty toiletry bag under his arm and stepped out into the hallway.

Hadley was already there, tucking fresh towels and sheets into the hall closet. Because of the narrow hallway, there wasn't any practical way to go around while she had the closet door open, so he waited.

She shut the door, saw him standing there and jumped. A little squeal escaped her lips.

He chuckled. "Sorry. Didn't mean to scare you, but the hall isn't wide enough for me to have gone around."

She put her hand on her chest, drew a few deep breaths. "No problem. I guess I'm just a bit of a nervous Nellie."

He sensed her tension and instinctively placed a hand on her shoulder. He could feel the stiffness gathered there. "Are you going to be okay?"

She looked up at him, those sparkling brown eyes of hers as wide as the plains in the Midwest. Her mouth fell open in an O shape, but she said nothing.

Something shifted between them as their eyes connected, and he sensed the tension leaving her, the muscles unknotting beneath his hand. "Am I making you uncomfortable?"

She shook her head, eyes still wide. "No."

He gave her shoulder a squeeze before moving his hand away.

Breaking the contact seemed to bring her back to the moment at hand. She blinked a few times, then asked, "Is there anything else you need me to do?"

"My laptop and the binders. I left them in the office. Could you grab them and bring them downstairs?"

She nodded. "Anything else?"

"The writing table up there. I'd like it moved into the downstairs bedroom, if it's not too heavy."

She was already headed toward the stairs. "Nah, I got it. That thing's not as heavy as it looks."

Over the next several minutes, she moved the writing table into the downstairs bedroom. Once she'd set it in the corner near the window, she placed his laptop and the three binders he'd brought with him on the table. He stood in the bedroom doorway, observing her.

She turned his way. "Are you good now?"

"Yes. Thanks for coming over to do this for me."

"You're welcome." Her brow cocked then. "What's going on with your back, anyway?"

He thought about what to say and about how much he wanted her to know. Not wanting her to think of him as helpless, he said, "Let's just say stunt work is hard on the body, and I'm not as young as I once was." *Great. Now I've made myself seem old.*

"Okay, then." She looked as if she wanted to know more, but thankfully, she didn't press. Moving toward him, she spoke again. "I'm headed home."

He moved so she could exit the bedroom, then trailed her to the door. "Thanks again, Hadley."

Opening the door, she turned back toward him with a smile. "Remember, if you need anything else, just call."

"Won't the office be closed over the weekend?"

A sly expression on her face, she reached into the pocket of her jeans and pulled out a business card. She moved into his personal space, adjusting his arm and hand until his palm was up and open, then pressed the card into his palm. "My cell phone number is on the back." Closing his fingers over the card, she slipped through the open door and closed it behind her.

As he flipped the card and read the number scrawled there, he couldn't contain his smile.

# Chapter 5

The interior of the Crowned by Curls salon bustled with activity Saturday morning as Hadley entered through the glass doors, with Belinda close behind her. Taking off her sunglasses and tucking them into her purse, Hadley wove her way across the carpeted waiting area to the reception desk.

"Damn, it's jumping in here today. Good thing we made appointments." Belinda ran her hand over her close-cropped hair. "I need my waves redone, like, yesterday."

Hadley chuckled. "Nobody tries to walk in here on a Saturday. At least, nobody who lives here." Only vacationers, operating on the assumption that a Black-owned salon in a small resort town could never be crowded, tried this.

Lisa, the desk clerk, smiled as the two women approached. She wore the hot-pink scrubs and black apron that constituted the salon's uniform. "What's up, Hadley? How you doing, Belinda?"

"We're good, girl." Belinda rested her elbows on the counter. "How the kids doing?"

Lisa rolled her eyes. "Girl, they're as rambunctious as ever."

"Y'all ready for us?"

Lisa winked. "You know how we roll here. You come on time for your appointment and we'll be ready. Go on back—they're waiting for y'all."

Circling around the desk, Hadley and Belinda passed through the beaded curtains to the back area of the salon, where the stylists maintained their stations. The fuchsia-painted walls of the salon were dressed with framed images of famous Black women. There were singers, actresses, educators and other luminaries of the race. The black-and-white tile floor hosted the ten stations for hairstylists, as well as four for nail technicians.

Sandra Jackson, the salon's owner and Hadley's personal stylist, waved her over to her station. Sandra, whose long, thin blond-highlighted dreadlocks were piled atop her head, ran a tight ship. "Hadley, come on over, girl. I'm ready for you."

Hadley waved to Belinda, who'd already slipped into Tammy's chair across the room, and climbed into Sandra's chair. "Hey, Sandra. How you doing?"

"Good, girl. Business is booming, and I can't complain." Picking up a wide-tooth comb, she attempted to sweep it through Hadley's loose curls. "Maybe I can complain. Girl, haven't you been detangling your hair?"

Hadley sucked at her bottom lip. "I have, but I didn't do it last night. And I fell asleep without my silk bonnet."

Sandra shook her head. "Tsk, tsk. I told you if you don't want to take care of your hair between visits, we can always shave your head." She gave Hadley's shoulder a gentle jab with the end of the comb.

Feeling properly chastised, Hadley shook her head. "No, no. I'll do better. I just want my usual wash and set. And I probably need a trim."

Sandra ran her fingers through her hair. "Yes, you do. Your ends are looking a little raggedy, girl. Let's get you to the shampoo bowl."

Once Hadley's tresses had been washed, trimmed and set on rollers, she sat underneath the hooded dryer. No sooner than she opened a magazine to pass the time, Belinda was ushered over and put beneath the dryer next to her.

The moment she was seated, Belinda spoke. "So, tell me. What's going on with that fine Devon Granger?"

Thanks to Sandra's investment in ultraquiet hair dryers, Hadley couldn't pretend not to have heard Belinda. Odds were most of the people in the back of the salon heard her, as well. "Pertaining to what, exactly?"

Belinda rolled her eyes. "Come on, girl. Did you ask him about Captain Vicious coming back for *DD3*?"

Hadley glanced around and noticed more than a few sets of eyes on her. Apparently, she and Belinda weren't the only ones curious about what to expect from the next film in the trilogy and the villain everyone loved to hate. "I did, but he's under a contract that says he can't tell anyone."

"So much for getting the scoop on that." Belinda leaned to her left a bit, as if trying to get closer to her friend. "Did you get any juicy Hollywood news out of him?"

She shook her head. "No filming and no premieres until after the New Year."

"Sheesh." Belinda popped her lips. "Well, let's get down to the real deal, then. Have you made your move on him yet?"

"Nice segue, B."

Belinda shrugged. "I do what I can. Now give me the dirt."

Hadley cocked her head to one side, hoping to redirect the hot air to a spot where her head felt more damp. "There's no dirt. At least, not yet."

"What are you waiting on? You had better make your move on him before some other woman does." Belinda tossed one leg over the other. "Remember, Sapphire Shores is a resort town. That means your competition is bigger than just the local girls. It's all the women traveling here as tourists, too."

Hadley sighed. She had history with Devon, and not just the past five Christmases spent seeing to his needs at the town house. They'd known each other since childhood, and while they'd never been more than friends in the past, she liked to think their long association counted for something. "True enough, but Devon and I have history."

"History, indeed. Your history is as the pip-squeak little sister, and his is as the hot friend of your older brother." Belinda chuckled. "Yeah. Y'all go way back."

Hadley stuck out her tongue at her friend. She loved Belinda like a sister, but sometimes she could do without her plainspoken honesty. "Thanks for the vote of confidence, B. If you feel that way about it, then why are you pushing me to go after him?"

"It's like I said. If you don't, someone else is going to move in on him."

Hadley fixed her with a glare and waited.

Belinda sighed. "Fine. Look, I've known you how long now? Approximately forever, right?"

"That's about right." They'd been the tag team of terror for more than a decade.

"In all that time, I've never known you to be into anyone the way you're into Devon. The way I see it, y'all are soul mates. I get that he's all famous now, and that makes it harder to approach him. But you're in a unique situation that gives you total access to him."

With her chin resting on her fist, Hadley nodded. "I suppose that's true. I even have a key to the town house…but I would never infringe on his privacy by using it without his permission."

"I'm not suggesting you do that. But I think it would be pretty stupid of you to let the opportunity to make your feelings known pass you by." Belinda's expression changed, becoming more serious. "I just want you to be happy, Hadley. You work so hard at MHI, picking up the slack for everyone else. You deserve to be happy, girl."

Despite her earlier annoyance, Hadley felt the smile

tipping her lips. "That's really sweet, B. Thanks for caring so much."

"Hey, somebody's got to look after you." Belinda playfully punched Hadley on the arm, an accompaniment to her teasing. "You're too busy looking out for everyone else."

Mulling her friend's words over, Hadley turned her attention back to the magazine still lying open across her lap. She continued to flip the pages and read some of the text, but her mind insisted on playing out possible ways she might approach Devon. She didn't want to come off as desperate or pushy or do anything else that would lead her efforts to crash and burn before they even got off the ground.

Her interactions with Devon so far made her aware of how much he valued his solitude and privacy. As much as she wanted to get his attention, she knew he wouldn't go for being openly pursued. No, it was best to bide her time and wait for the right moment to let him know exactly how she felt.

Somehow, she knew that moment was coming.

With his tablet in hand, Devon slid open the glass doors leading to the back patio. The stone courtyard, with its resin-and-glass dining set, gas grill and comfortable resin love seat, was one of his favorite features of the town house. The location of the property, near the southern tip of the island, meant he could enjoy ocean views from both the front and back of the house. He eased onto the cushioned love seat and settled in. Just beyond the five-foot powder-coated iron fence surrounding the patio lay a wide band of sand that gave way to the blue waves of the Atlantic.

He turned his attention to the tablet, adjusting the screen brightness for easier viewing in the sunlight. The day was temperate, in the midfifties, and he'd donned a pair of gray sweatpants and a long-sleeved black T-shirt. Usually at this time on a Saturday afternoon, he'd be working out, but his injury prevented him from doing much in the way of exercise other than walking. The prescription he'd gotten from Dr. Stinger did a lot to ease the pain, but he didn't want to risk making matters worse by hitting the gym.

He took a deep breath, inhaling the fresh air. As he exhaled, he made sure to force the air out from his diaphragm. Despite his inability to do his usual number of sit-ups, he was determined to maintain his core strength. He was no doctor, but he knew that abdominal strength and stability would only help his back.

He tapped the screen, intent on opening the web browser, but an incoming video call interrupted his effort. Seeing the face of his old friend and mentor on the screen made him smile. Swiping across, he answered the call. "Rick! How the hell are you?"

"Great, great. How are you doing, young buck?" Rick Rollingsworth, a consummate actor who was considered Hollywood royalty, smiled from across the miles. The man was in great physical shape, and the only hint of his nearly sixty years of living was the small streak of gray hair running across his hairline. "Enjoying your vacation?"

"Yes. It's beautiful down here. And far more quiet

than LA could ever be." Devon raised the tablet, turn-ing it so Rick could see the water. "Look at that ocean. And barely a soul out here to disturb my peace."

Rick chuckled. "I'm jealous. I'm still on set for the Teddy Pendergrass biopic." He panned his camera around, showing Devon the bustling activity going on in the studio. An outdoor backdrop, depicting a city street, hung behind Rick. People rushed back and forth through the cavernous space, carrying props, chatting noisily and pushing carts. "They're moving equipment between soundstages right now, then they'll set up the next take."

Devon shook his head. He admired Rick's work ethic, and he knew a large part of Rick's success as an African American actor in a less-than-hospitable film industry could be traced back to it. "Jeez. It's little more than a week before Christmas. When are they gonna wrap this thing up?"

"Hell if I know." Rick shrugged. "Filming is going to continue in the New Year, probably. But I expect they'll let us go for a holiday break in the next couple of days. Even if they don't, I'm out by the twentieth. My wife isn't going to have me staying any longer than that."

"How is Odetta, anyway? I haven't seen her in a while." Devon was particularly fond of Rick's wife, who loved to bake and often sent cookies, pies and other homemade sweets to the film sets they worked on together.

"She's great. She's out shopping right now, no doubt. Between her and Richelle, I gotta take most of the roles that come my way." He laughed as he spoke of his twentysomething daughter, his and Odetta's only child. "They're both spoiled as hell, but I wouldn't have it any other way."

Devon chuckled. "We both know that. So, what's up? There's got to be a reason you're calling me from on set."

Rick snapped his fingers, as if remembering something. "Yes, there is. I've been called to consult on a new film project. The screenwriter wants to put together a whole new team of up-and-coming talent. You know, a new director, producer, actors at the beginning of their careers, the whole nine."

Devon's ears perked up. "Really? So, what's the project about?"

"It's a romantic thriller, exploring the Black Panther Party in the '60s. I've seen the script, and it's pretty impressive writing. The man's got a gift, and if he can pull the right team together, he's got a hit on his hands."

Scratching his chin, Devon thought about what he'd just heard. The film's premise was intriguing, and he always sought out roles that allowed him to tell stories he thought were important. "How are the Panthers portrayed?"

"Pretty objectively, from what I can tell. You won't find any of that manufactured lore about them being a criminal organization, but they aren't painted as saints, either."

The more Devon heard, the more he liked the project. "So, I guess this means you're ready to deal me in, then?"

Rick nodded. "Yeah. I thought you might like to step

in as one of the Panthers' enforcers. The role is available, and you've definitely got the body type."

Devon sucked in a breath. "Okay, Rick. I'm interested in participating, but not as an actor."

Rick's thick brow rose a few inches. "Then what, pray tell, would you be doing?"

"Directing." He kept his expression even, hoping to convey his seriousness.

It was to no avail, because Rick immediately burst out laughing.

Devon sat there, watching the screen and waiting for Rick to recover.

When he finally stopped laughing, he said, "Okay, Devon. I'll let the screenwriter know that everyone's favorite action hero wants to direct."

Devon frowned. "Come on, Rick. I'm serious."

That only started the laughter again. "I hear you, man." Rick inserted his words between guffaws. "Look, I'll let you go. I'll get back to you on your directorial debut. 'Bye, Devon." His image faded from the screen as he ended the video call.

Setting the tablet on the cushion next to him, Devon folded his arms over his chest. He'd put himself out there, made his aspirations known, only to be laughed at by the man he looked up to.

He shook his head ruefully. This was precisely why he hadn't told anyone of his aspirations. Moving behind the camera wasn't some fly-by-night idea he'd come up with on the plane ride. He'd been thinking about it for the past two years, at least. He loved acting and loved his fans even more. But the stunt work side of things only became harder and more physically taxing as the years went by. He wasn't foolish enough to think he'd stay young and able-bodied forever. Even though he kept himself in excellent physical shape, his efforts hadn't prevented his recent injury.

All he could do now was wait and hope Rick put in a good word for him. With no information on the project other than the general premise, he'd be hard-pressed to find out any more about it on his own.

His face tight with tension and worry, Devon closed his eyes and set his focus on the sound of the rolling waves.

# Chapter 6

Standing in line at Della's Delicatessen, Hadley tapped her foot to the rhythm of an '80s pop song playing on the jukebox. There were still three people ahead of her, as well as five or six behind her. She'd been waiting about ten minutes so far, but this wasn't anything new for the Monday lunch rush. There were no other delis in town, so if you wanted a great sandwich that you didn't have to make yourself, you stood in line at Della's with everybody else.

Once the person ahead of her was served, she moved forward in time with the rest of the line. Her phone buzzed in the hip pocket of her slacks, and she reached to check it.

It was a text message from Belinda.

Lunch today?

She typed a quick reply.

Can't. Grabbing lunch for the office. TTYL.

Sending the message off, she tucked her phone away just as the line moved again. Observing the faces of the people around her, she saw many that were familiar. Della's was an out-of-the-way spot, tucked in a nondescript one-story building on the southwestern side of the island. Only the intrepid tourist in search of a quick lunch or light dinner found the place, which was a hit among the locals. There were several chain restaurants that were more centrally located, and Hadley had driven right past them on her way to Della's.

When Hadley got to the counter, the woman herself greeted her. Della Hall, her gray hair covered in her signature white hairnet, leaned over the counter as she approached. "Hey, Hadley. How are you? How are your parents and those crazy brothers of yours?"

Smiling, Hadley set her purse on the counter. "Everybody's good, Della. You ready for the holidays?"

"Yes, if you mean ready to take myself a vacation. We close up on the twenty-third and don't open back up until the second of January."

"Here's the order, Miss Della." A young man in one of Della's famous green-checked aprons passed her two plastic bags brimming with food.

"Thank you." Della placed the bags on the counter in

front of Hadley. "Okay, love. Got your order right here. Let's run through it and make sure everything's there."

Hadley ran down the office lunch order, which included seven different sandwiches, a salad and all the side items. The fridge in the break room was usually stocked with drinks, so she'd left those off when she had called in the order earlier. As Hadley went down the list, Della produced each item from one of the bags. "Looks like we're all set." She passed Della the company credit card.

After Della swiped the card, she handed it back to Hadley with her receipt. "There you go. Y'all enjoy."

"Thanks, Della." Hoisting the two bags down from the counter, Hadley turned and started to leave.

"Wait a minute. Let me ask you something."

She turned back to face Della. "Sure. What is it?"

"Any word on what y'all are going to do with that last plot of land you just cleared?" Della tapped the end of a short pencil on the counter as she waited for a response.

Hadley shook her head. "Not yet, but there's a meeting about that after lunch. Whatever I find out, I'll pass on to you."

"I'd appreciate it. If it's possible, I'd love to build a bigger deli, and that's about the only place left on the island where I can do it."

Hadley nodded. "I'll look into it and let you know." With that, she took the food and exited the deli. Outside, she set the bags on the passenger floorboard of the company car, climbed in and drove away.

Back at the office, she hoisted the bags out of the car. At first, she thought she'd be hauling them in, but one of the two young male interns from Campbell's department helped her bring everything in and set it down in the break room. Campbell had only had his interns for about three weeks, and Hadley wondered when he'd start putting them to full use. Maybe then he'd stop leaving his work on her desk. After thanking the young man, she claimed her salad box and took it to her office to eat at her desk.

After lunch, she filed into the conference room with her brothers and the five other staff members who normally attended these meetings. Savion, as chief executive, sat at the head of the table, with Campbell to his right and Hadley to his left. The receptionist, marketing officer, operations officer and the two interns rounded out the group.

Once everyone had settled into their seats, Savion stood and grabbed a long tube of paper that had been leaning against the wall behind his chair. "Good afternoon, everyone. I called this meeting to share with you an interesting proposal that has come in for the remaining land MHI plans to develop." He unfastened the band around the paper and opened it, rolling it out on the table.

Campbell, poring over the paper with the others, asked, "What is it?"

"This is a concept drawing for Sapphire Landing. It would be a place designed specifically for the convenience of the tourists who visit Sapphire Shores."

Staring at the oversize paper to view the drawing, Hadley could feel her brow furrowing. "It looks like a mall. All I see is a bunch of chain stores and restaurants clustered together."

Savion shook his head. "No. It's not a mall. While there is shopping available from familiar brands, there are also condominiums. We could rent them out at a premium price because of their proximity to restaurants, shopping and the beach."

Hadley frowned. From what she could see, the whole thing looked and sounded gaudy and overly commercial. Savion seemed to have dollar signs where his pupils should be, and she was afraid that he couldn't hear what she was saying over the sound of the imaginary cash register ringing in his head. "What happened to donating some of the land to the municipality for public green space? Or offering plots to local businesses that want to relocate and expand?" She thought about Della and her desire to grow her business. In a prime location, Della would do very well.

Martin, the marketing officer, piped up then. "There's still the possibility of that. We all know that donating land would only benefit our public image."

Hadley sighed. Martin was the only one who'd offered any defense of the green space idea, and it had been solely based on building up the company's reputation, not on building up the community for the island's residents. She turned to her older brother. "Savion. This development is all wrong for our island. It just doesn't fit the way we live here."

"And what brings you to that conclusion, Hadley?" The condescension had already begun to creep into his tone.

Struggling to keep her frustration with him in check, she answered, "We're a close-knit community, and I think bringing in all these chains and fancy condominiums will diminish the special charm of Sapphire Shores."

Savion shook his head. "You're so young and idealistic, Hadley. It isn't just about the money we'll make on this deal. Think of all the new jobs this would bring to the island. Construction jobs at first, then jobs within the establishments once they're open."

At the opposite end of the table, the receptionist, who'd been busy taking notes, glanced up on the heels of his words. As if sensing the rising tension, she immediately turned her attention back to her laptop.

Hadley pursed her lips. Her brother had just dismissed her, again, and everyone in the room could sense it. Leaning back in her chair, she vowed to keep quiet the rest of the meeting. Arguing with Savion was about as effective as arguing with a telephone pole. As the rest of the staff talked excitedly about what it would be like to have a place like Sapphire Landing in town, she tuned them out. Her focus was better spent on coming up with a way to stop this development and formulating an alternate plan for the land.

She loved Sapphire Shores. She stayed because she loved this place.

And she wouldn't sit idly by and watch some developer ruin everything that made it unique.

Tuesday afternoon, Devon was sitting sideways on the couch with his feet propped up on the backrest. The television was on, but he wasn't really watching it. He'd spent the better part of the day calling around to see if any agency could send over a housekeeper or personal chef to handle his meals.

His search had been largely fruitless, since Quick Transformations was the only agency on the island that handled such requests. He supposed he understood that, as there was probably very little call for personal chefs in Sapphire Shores. Since Quick Transformations already provided housekeeping for MHI, he'd thought he might be able to request some extra service.

"We'd love to help you, Mr. Granger," the receptionist had told him. "But I'm afraid our staff is already greatly reduced this time of year. We'll be closing in a few days and won't reopen until after the New Year."

With a sigh, he readjusted his position as he tried to come up with a way around this little problem. He'd already tried to cook for himself, against Dr. Stinger's advice. That had been a colossal mistake that had led to him having to take an extra dose of the painkiller he'd been prescribed. Standing in one spot for more than a few minutes was simply not going to happen again, at least not without pain.

He'd been in town a little less than a week now and had already grown tired of takeout food. What he wanted was a home-cooked meal, as many of them as he could get. Obviously, he wasn't going to be the one doing the cooking, and therein lay his dilemma.

He looked at his phone lying on the coffee table in front of him. Hadley popped into his mind. She had said to call her if he needed anything. Cooking for him seemed to be well outside her job description, but then again, so had rearranging things in the town house. She'd come over and done that without any complaints.

Contemplating his options, he realized he didn't really have anyone else to call. He'd have to walk a fine line between asking her for help and burdening her. He knew Hadley was already busy with things at MHI, and he didn't want her to think he was taking advantage simply because she'd made herself available to him.

In the end, logic won out, and he gave Hadley a call.

"Hello?"

"Hi, Hadley. It's Devon."

With a smile in her voice, she asked, "Do you need something?"

He took a deep breath. "Yes. I have kind of an unorthodox request."

"More unorthodox than rearranging the town house?"

He chuckled. "I'm afraid so."

"I'm listening."

"I'm not supposed to be standing on my feet for long periods of time. That's fine, since I'm on vacation, but it does leave me with a problem."

"What's that?"

"I can't cook. I've got a refrigerator full of groceries here, and no way to indulge my love of cooking."

"I'd hate for it all to go bad."

"So would I, since I paid for it." A nervous laugh left his throat, and he decided to just come out with his request. "I know you're busy at the office, but I'm tired of eating takeout. Is there any way you could cook for me? It doesn't have to be every day, and you don't have to come here and do it. Since I'm asking you for a favor, I'll let you decide the parameters."

The line was silent for a few moments.

Was she thinking it over? Or had they been disconnected? "Are you still there?"

She laughed. "Yes. I'm just trying to decide what I'll cook first."

He felt the smile stretching his lips. "So, you'll do it?"

"Sure. It's not a problem if I can cook what I'm already making for myself. I'll just double my recipes, and voilà, your problem is solved."

"When could you start?"

"How about tonight? I was going to make Chinese, and I don't mind coming over there."

He felt his nervousness dissipate, replaced by the anticipation of her presence. "I have just about everything here. Whoever did the shopping was very thorough."

"Sounds good. I'll just bring over some spices, and we should be good to go." She paused. "You realize you're going to have to tell me the entire truth about what's going on with your back, right?"

"Yes. If you're willing to do all this for me, I owe you that much." He reclined against the backrest of the sofa. "I'll tell you the whole story tonight over dinner. How's that?"

She sounded pleased. "Then I'll see you tonight around seven. 'Bye, Devon."

"'Bye." He disconnected the call and set his phone aside. His eyes focused on the view through the patio doors, he wondered what tonight would hold. He'd be out of his mind to deny the attraction sparking between them. Would it all come to a head tonight?

He didn't know, but he planned to let things progress naturally. Wherever that led, he'd be ready.

## Chapter 7

Hadley knocked on the door of the town house at a few minutes past seven. With a paper grocery bag balanced on her hip, she waited, marching in place to stay warm. The temperature had dropped after the sun went down and the chilly day faded into a cold December night.

Devon swung open the door, greeting her with a smile. "Hi, Hadley."

His lips continued to move, as if he were saying something more. But everything he said after his initial greeting went unheard as her eyes raked over him. She hadn't intended on staring at him, but she couldn't help it. He wore a closely fitted long-sleeved black T-shirt that displayed the outline of the ripped upper body beneath. Charcoal-gray slacks encased his powerful thighs and legs. A thick gold rope chain hanging around his neck suspended the head of a roaring lion in the center of his chest.

*How can he be this fine?* Every time she saw him, her brain shut down. When it came to concentrating in Devon's presence, the struggle was quite real.

"Hadley, did you hear me?" He touched her arm. "Come on inside out of the cold."

His velvet voice brought her back to reality, and her awareness of the frigid air swirling around her returned. She offered a crooked smile to her amused host. "Thanks."

He stepped aside to allow her in. Once she was inside the town house, she carried the paper bag to the kitchen while he locked up. Setting the bag on the counter, she removed the supplies she'd brought over to supplement Devon's grocery stockpile.

He entered the kitchen, and she felt his presence the moment he did. Her nose twitched as she detected the familiar woodsy fragrance of his cologne. "You look nice tonight, Hadley."

"Thank you." She'd donned a green turtleneck sweater dress, black leggings and tall black boots to work this morning, and had come straight to the town house from the office. She arranged the sesame oil, sesame seeds, soy sauce and rice wine vinegar she'd brought on the counter, trying not to get too excited about his compliment.

A tremor shot through her as he moved closer. He entered her space, standing directly behind her as he placed his fingertips on her shoulder. "Thank you again for doing this. I really do appreciate it."

Her conversation with Belinda in the salon came to mind, and she remembered her decision to seize the opportunity with Devon when the moment was right. Standing there, with his warm breath on the back of her neck, she knew what she needed to do. Drawing a deep breath, she turned around to face him. "Before I start cooking, can we talk for a minute?"

He nodded, backing up a bit. Leaning his hips against the opposite counter, he looked her way. "Sure. What's on your mind?"

This was the moment she'd been waiting for. For the last four years, she'd been waiting to tell him how she felt, never planning a speech. She just wanted to speak from her heart. "I don't want you to think I'm just being friendly and helpful by doing this."

His thick brow cocked upward. "Oh, really?"

She nodded. Maintaining eye contact with him was something of a struggle, but she refused to look away until she'd said what was on her heart. "I...have feelings for you. Strong feelings that tell me I want to be more than just your friend."

His expression remained unchanged, revealing nothing about his reaction. "And how long have you been feeling this way?"

She hesitated. *Maybe I should have come up with a speech.* "At least three years. Maybe longer. But I know you're a widower, and I wanted to be respectful of your grief."

He straightened then, taking a few steps, which brought him back into her personal space. "That's very considerate." He reached out then, his fingertips grazing down the sleeve of her dress until he clasped her hand in his own.

Her heart jumped into her throat as she realized he was receptive. Drawing her bottom lip into her mouth, she lowered her gaze. She didn't know what else to say. Thankfully, it appeared she wouldn't need to say anything else.

He squeezed her hand. "I'm honored that you feel this way about me, Hadley." He raised her hand, lifting it to his lips. Brushing a kiss over her knuckles, he set his golden eyes on her face. "You're an attractive, intelligent and caring woman, and I'm very open to seeing what we could have."

Her breath escaped in a rush, then a wide grin broke over her face.

His smile melted her heart. "Are you still cooking?"

Laughing, she nodded. "Yes. We still have to eat, right?"

"I suppose." He released her hand, gesturing to the stove. "I'll leave you to it."

She took a few deep breaths to settle herself before her hormones got the better of her. Then she went back to the sink to wash her hands.

He strolled to the dining room table and took a seat. The open layout of the town house meant there was no wall separating the kitchen from the other common rooms on the first floor. "I think I'll stay here and keep you company while you cook, if you don't mind."

"I don't mind at all." Concentration be damned, she loved having him nearby. With him sitting at the table only a few feet from her, she started to cook.

Within the hour, the kitchen was filled with the savory aromas of the dishes she'd begun to prepare. One skillet held the cornstarch-battered chicken, frying in a shallow bath of vegetable oil. The other held baby peas, diced carrots and chopped onions, sizzling in oil along with cooked brown rice.

"Smells fantastic in here. What are we having?" Devon leaned forward, resting his elbows on the surface of the table.

"Sesame chicken, fried rice and egg rolls." She looked at the digital display to check the oven temperature. Satisfied that it had heated up enough, she slid in the waiting sheet pan.

"I'm impressed. I've never had homemade sesame chicken."

"You'll love it." She tucked the cutting boards she'd used to dice the chicken and onions into the dishwasher. After washing her hands again, she grabbed a paper towel from the standing dispenser to dry her hands before chucking it into the trash. "Or at least I hope so. It's hard work making this stuff from scratch, though I did use precooked brown rice."

He chuckled. "Nothing wrong with a shortcut now and then." He stood then, slowly making his way back into the kitchen.

She watched him, feeling her heartbeat hasten as he approached. "Shouldn't you be resting your back, Devon?"

"I promised to tell you the problem, and I'm telling you now. I have a herniated disk near my tailbone.

That's why I need to take it easy and stay off the second floor."

Concern swept over her, and she resisted the urge to chastise him or try to force him to sit back down. "Are you sure you should be on your feet right now?"

A wicked smile lit his face as he came abreast of her. "I'm fine. Now, like I was saying. A shortcut is okay now and again, but not when it comes to us."

She noticed his quick change of subject but chose not to address it. "What do you mean?" She trembled as his nearness threatened to overwhelm her.

He placed his palms on her arms. Though she was encased in the dress, his touch seemed to penetrate the fabric.

"There won't be any shortcuts with me and you. I want to get to know you, and I want to take my time doing it." He leaned low, his face mere inches from hers. "No shortcuts."

"Mmm." It was the only sound she could manage. She looked into his hazel eyes and felt her insides melt.

Hooking his finger beneath her chin, he whispered, "Can I?"

She didn't need an illustration to know what he was asking. "Please do."

She saw him smile as he tilted her face to an angle more to his liking. Seconds later, his lips touched hers, and her eyes closed as the sweetness spread through her like wildfire. His lips were soft, and she relished the feeling of them. None of her fantasies matched this fiery reality. He kissed her solidly yet gently, lingering for a few long moments before easing away.

Only the sizzling of the food on the stove broke the silent aftermath as she stared into his eyes.

*He is one hell of a man.*

Tuesday afternoon, Devon sat on a padded stool at the bar inside the Salty Siren. He'd been coming there every year since he started vacationing in Sapphire Shores for the holidays, and he loved the food, the top-shelf drinks and the laid-back atmosphere. There was always a game on the television, plus all the giant chicken wings you could eat and a great selection of beers on tap. Holiday decorations consisted of several wreaths fashioned from beer can tabs and a single four-foot Christmas tree occupying the corner behind the hostess stand.

He'd decided to break the cabin fever that had begun to set in by meeting his old friend Campbell for a quick chat. Even as he stared absently at the highlight reel on the television in front of him, he couldn't shake his memories of the previous night.

When Hadley had revealed her feelings to him, he hadn't been surprised. He'd mostly been pleased, flattered and happy that she'd decided to make a move. He still held on to some nervousness about dating his friend's younger sister. But the kisses they'd shared last night made it clear that he had no choice but to give in to the attraction between them. Like the pots of food on the stove last night when they'd shared that initial kiss, the feelings had been simmering for a long time and had finally reached their boiling point.

Campbell, who'd been sitting on the stool next to him

for the past fifteen minutes or so, perused the laminated menu. "I get the same thing every time I come here."

Brought back to reality, Devon shrugged. "If it ain't broke…"

Chuckling, Campbell laid the menu on the bar. "You're right. I'm just gonna order the wings."

By then, the bartender in the fitted T-shirt bearing the namesake Salty Siren sidled up. The blue-eyed brunette had been openly flirting with Devon ever since he and Campbell had entered. She leaned over the bar in front of him, the V-neck of her shirt revealing her ample bust. "What can I get ya, Mr. Granger?"

Giving her the practiced smile he gave all his overzealous fans, he replied, "Call me Devon."

She sighed. "I'd just as soon call you handsome. Did I mention how much I loved *Reach for the Sky*?"

Campbell rolled his eyes. "Yes, twice. You do see me sitting here, right, Maddie?"

She cut her eyes in his direction. "Yeah, I see you. And I know you want teriyaki wings and a Blue Moon. You order the same thing every time you come in here."

Devon hid his amusement as he watched the exchange.

"You're coming off a little salty today, Maddie." Campbell folded his arms over his chest. "You can't be acting up just because we went to school together. Expect that to be reflected in your tip."

*Did we go to school together?* Devon searched his memory bank for a Maddie in his graduating class but came up empty of one that fit her description.

She giggled and stuck out her tongue at him. "Whatever." Smoothly switching her focus back to Devon, she continued, "It isn't every day we get a bona fide celebrity in here."

Devon waved his hand in a show of modesty. "You're too kind. But I'll have the chicken nachos and a Sprite, please."

"Coming right up." Maddie winked at him as she walked away.

"No beer today?" Campbell asked.

"Nah. Mixes with my pain meds, and I gotta drive myself back to the town house."

Maddie placed a tall glass of iced soda in front of him, then set a frosty bottle of beer in front of Campbell. Tossing another grin in Devon's direction, she moved away.

"I feel ya." Campbell relaxed his arms, resting his elbows on the bar. "Meanwhile, looks like Maddie's trying to get with you, man."

Devon shook his head. "Not interested."

Campbell's eyebrow cocked. "What? You're not down with the swirl? I'm shocked, with you coming from Hollyweird and all."

Devon gave his buddy a punch on the shoulder. "Shut up, Cam. It's not that. There's somebody else."

"Oh, really? Who?"

Hesitating for a beat, he replied, "Your sister."

Shock registered on Campbell's face, and he shifted positions on the stool so he faced Devon. "What? When did this happen?"

"Last night."

Face scrunched into a frown, Campbell shook his head. "Bro."

Realizing his error, Devon chuckled. "No, no. It's not like that."

"It better not be."

"I should rephrase." He'd wanted to be honest with his friend, but it hadn't come across the way he'd intended. "Last night, Hadley told me that she's been attracted to me for a while, and honestly, I've been interested in her, too."

Campbell asked, "And what does that mean?"

"It means we're going to take our time getting to know each other better."

That seemed to satisfy him, at least to a degree. His shoulders dropped, and he turned back toward the bar. "Okay then. That sounds a lot better."

Devon watched his friend, gauging his reaction. "So, does that mean you're okay with this?"

Campbell looked him in the eye. "Your playboy days are over, right?"

"Those ended years ago, before I married Natalie."

He shrugged. "Then it's cool with me."

"Really?"

"Hadley's grown. It's not really my place to interfere."

He nodded, taking in the response. It was lukewarm, neither for or against. The more he thought about it, the more he realized it was just typical Campbell, one of the most laid-back dudes he'd ever known.

"My only request is this—don't hurt my sister. If you do, we fighting."

"Understood." Devon expected nothing less, because if he hurt her, he deserved a swift kick.

"I'm not the one you should be worried about, though. Savion's the one who's always trying to tell Hadley what to do." Campbell chuckled. "She usually does what she wants anyway, but that's never stopped him from trying."

Devon let out a chuckle of his own, one fueled by his nerves. He hadn't given much thought to Savion, the oldest Monroe sibling. Odds were Savion wouldn't take too kindly to Devon dating his baby sister. "He's probably not going to like it. But I don't intend on letting Savion tell me what to do, either."

Maddie returned with their food then, sliding the plates in front of them.

Digging into his wings, Campbell smiled. "I'm actually looking forward to Savion's reaction to all this. Should be pretty entertaining."

Devon couldn't help laughing at that. "Hopefully we won't have to square up." He picked up his soda and took a long drink.

"And if it came to that?" Campbell's eyes widened as he awaited an answer.

Setting the glass down, Devon looked his friend right in the eye. "Then it's on. She's worth it." He meant every word. He'd had his share of liaisons with women, and he could see Hadley's worth. It was all over her, glowing as brightly as a neon sign on a moonless night.

Campbell nodded, his expression showing his approval. "My man." He offered his fist.

Bumping fists with Campbell, Devon settled in to his seat and dug in to his meal.

# Chapter 8

Wednesday afternoon, Hadley arrived at Oceanview Grill at a few minutes past noon. The OG, as the locals called it, was known all over the island for its top-quality seafood prepared on a wood-fired grill. She inhaled the delicious woodsy aroma as she strolled up to the hostess stand and gave her name. Hadley had arrived first, so she followed the hostess to a booth near the rear of the restaurant, situated beneath a large window.

Settling into the soft brown leather cushion, Hadley picked up one of the two menus the hostess had left on the lacquered wood table. It took her only a few moments to select the day's special: mesquite salmon with braised brussels sprouts and mushroom risotto. Laying the menu back down, she directed her attention to the view outside the window. The temperature had risen into the sixties today, but the hazy gray sky heralded a coming rainstorm. The restaurant's perch on a hill overlooking the sand dunes and the Atlantic on the southeastern tip of the island gave it a beautiful view. She stared out to where the water seemed to rise to meet the sky, sighing contentedly.

*I don't know which is better here—the food or the atmosphere.*

Voices and footsteps near the entrance drew her attention to a view almost as breathtaking as the one outside the window. When she turned her head, she saw Devon approaching the table. He wore a white button-down shirt, dark denim jeans and black moccasins. The top two buttons of the shirt were undone, giving her a view of the powerful, muscled lines of his neck and upper chest. A pair of dark sunglasses were tucked in his shirt pocket. His hazel eyes swept the restaurant's interior until they landed on her. Then his soft, full lips turned up in a smile that threatened to be her undoing.

He walked up to the table. "Hello, Hadley. You look beautiful."

She felt the warmth filling her cheeks. "Hi, Devon. And, thank you."

He slipped into the booth, sliding over until he was in the center of the bench. "Have you been waiting long?"

She shook her head. "Just a few minutes. The waiter hasn't even been by yet."

He picked up his menu, opening the laminated pages.

She watched the way his large hands grasped the menu, her mind drifting toward other things he might grip with both hands. How would his hands feel holding her hips that way? And just like that, the familiar tingle rose again. It started at the base of her spine and snaked its way up until the hairs on the back of her neck stood on end. What was it about Devon that put her in this state? He made her feel like an enamored teenager.

"What will you be having today, Miss Monroe?" The waiter's question drew Hadley back to the present moment.

Clearing her throat, she passed him the menu. "I'll have the daily special, please. And an iced tea." Looking down at the table, she saw the two glasses of ice water and a basket of rolls that had materialized while she'd been lost in her own thoughts.

Devon handed over his menu, as well. "I'd like the same, with root beer, please."

After the waiter left them alone, she turned her attention back to Devon. Thinking of him that way made her smile. "So, how's your back today?"

"It's feeling pretty good. I've done my stretches, and I'm taking my meds and staying off the second floor as instructed." He rested his elbows on the table and laced his long fingers together. "I see you're still looking out for me."

"Now more than ever." She winked.

"I think it's really sweet." Separating his fingers, he reached out and captured her hands in his. "Now, tell me what's on your mind." His golden eyes locked with hers.

*Should I tell him I'm thinking of what it would be like to have him touch me?* Her mind wandered back to that night two years ago, when they'd almost kissed. Belinda had stealthily hung a sprig of mistletoe by the front door of the town house, and Hadley had come over to drop off a batch of Christmas cookies from her mom. He'd said something about tradition, and leaned in, but before she could even pucker, the damn sprig fell off the doorframe and landed on the floor. Her cheeks had been so hot, she must have been twelve shades of red as she'd made her hasty retreat.

Thinking of that now made her feel awkward, so she decided against bringing it up.

She blinked a few times as she became aware of his scrutiny. "I…uh…" Yes, they were dating now, but she felt their relationship was a little too new for her to unleash her intense physical desire on him. No, it would be better to tell him about the other thing weighing on her mind. "There's another developer vying to purchase the land we just cleared. It's the last tract of Monroe family land on the island. We have our own plans, but now things are up in the air."

His brow creased. "What developer? And what do they want the land for?"

She sighed. "The company is called Neville South, and they want to build a tacky, oversize mall filled with nothing but chain stores."

"No room for local businesses to rent shops there, I'm guessing?"

"None. You seem familiar with this type of thing."

He shrugged. "I see it in LA all the time. Company swoops in, buys land, pushes folks out and slaps up some pretentious commercial center."

She snapped her fingers. "Yes. Exactly that. The only

difference is no one lives there, so it seems like an easy, mess-free land grab for Neville South."

He shook his head. "Wow. How do your brothers feel about the offer?"

She rolled her eyes. "Campbell isn't going to say anything one way or the other—that's just how he is. But Savion is basically ready to sign the land over."

"Why would he do that?" His face showed genuine confusion.

"Because as part of the deal, Neville South will build some upscale condominiums. They would take on all the building costs, but let MHI collect the rental fees and handle the maintenance." She could imagine how excited her brother had been to hear that part of the deal. The idea of collecting fees on a property MHI didn't pay to build probably made Savion want to break-dance. The company did far more business in real estate, partly because of the overhead involved in property development.

"It's obvious you're not down with this offer."

"That's an understatement." She frowned. "I hate everything about it." She stopped, realizing how negative she sounded. "I don't want to drag you down with this stuff, Devon."

"You're not." He gave her hands a squeeze. "This is bothering you, and I want to hear about it."

She smiled, despite the bad feelings that had been brought up by talking about Neville South. Gazing into his beautiful eyes, she could see his concern, and that made her comfortable enough to go on. "I've lived here most of my life, and I stayed after college even though I had offers to go elsewhere. I love this island, and I know this development will ruin everything that makes it special. Denying the chance for expansion to our local businesses…increasing traffic from the mainland as people flock to these chain stores…more trash… There are so many reasons I oppose it."

"You're pretty fired up about this. Now the question is, what are you going to do about it?" He watched her, awaiting her response.

Shrugging, she replied, "I don't know if there's anything I can do."

He gave her a crooked grin. "Come on now. MHI is your family's company. If you really want to stop this development from happening, I'm sure there's something you can do."

"But what?" She genuinely didn't know how she could impact the outcome. "Talking to Savion is like talking to a brick wall, and Campbell's too busy avoiding work to care."

"You say you can't talk to Savion." He fixed her with a direct, telling look. "Try going over his head." He released her hands to make room on the table for the plates the waiter brought.

She mulled over his words. *I wonder what Mom and Dad would have to say about this deal?*

As they each took their respective plates, Devon stole glances at Hadley. She looked beautiful in the black turtleneck and long denim skirt she wore. Her hair was swept up into a ponytail.

They shared most of the meal in companionable

quiet. By the time dessert came, he found that he couldn't tear his eyes away from her.

He watched her lift a forkful of strawberry short-cake to her lips. She opened her mouth, tucked the cake inside and chewed gracefully. Her eyes closed, and a soft groan escaped her throat. The look of pleasure that came over her face affected him more than he would ever have expected.

She'd only expressed her feelings the night before, and already, he was prepared to act on them. The truth was, she wasn't the only one with feelings. If he were honest, her admission had given him permission to act on his own attraction to her. It hadn't always been there, because he'd loved Natalie with all his heart. But as time had passed, putting more and more distance between the loss of his wife and the present, his pain had also less-ened, making room for him to notice Hadley's appeal.

He started eating but continued to watch Hadley be-tween bites. She continued to wear that blissful ex-pression, giving away her enjoyment of the meal. He wanted to put that look on her face and give her all the pleasure she deserved. But he knew better than to say something like that aloud at this stage in a relationship, most of all in public.

So he grabbed his glass and took a long swig, will-ing the icy root beer to cool his hormones as well as his throat. Needing to make conversation to break the ten-sion, he asked, "Did talking about your concerns make you feel a little better?"

She nodded, taking a sip of her tea. "It did. Thanks."

"No problem." He felt good about helping her on their first official date.

Laying her fork across her nearly empty plate, she sat back on the bench. "You know, I'm just thinking. Even though we're just starting out on this relationship journey, I feel really comfortable with you."

He nodded. "I agree. I think it's because we started out being friends. You've always been chatty and sweet to me whenever I came into town." Unable to resist the urge to tease her, he winked. "Last night I found out why."

She laughed, shaking her head. "Oh, hush, Devon. You know we've always had good chemistry." She hesitated a moment before her next statement. "I feel like I can trust you."

He smiled. "You can."

"Do you feel that way about me?"

"Yes. Everything about you tells me you can be trusted." He pushed aside his own clean plate, settling his focus on her.

"Good. So now that we've settled that, what's on your mind? Maybe I can help you out the way you helped me." She leaned forward again, indicating her interest in whatever he said next.

He thought about his aspirations to direct. No one knew about them except Rick Rollingsworth, and Devon wasn't entirely sure Rick had taken him seriously. And even though he sensed Hadley wasn't the type to make fun of his dreams, he still wasn't quite ready to tell her about that, at least not in detail. "I've been thinking about making a change in my career."

She looked thoughtful for a moment. "Oh, you mean not doing your own stunts anymore? You did say it's hard on the body."

*I did say that.* Since he didn't want to go into the complexities of his plans, he went along with what she'd mentioned. "Yes. I'm not really into stunt work the way I once was. It's time for me to move on."

"I totally understand, and I agree. I mean, look at all those other big-name actors who don't do their own stunts but still make a killing doing action films." She folded her arms over her chest. "There's no reason you should sacrifice your physical well-being for your work."

"You're right. I've already spoken to Rick Rollingsworth about a possible project, one that could take my career in a whole new direction."

A bright smile spread across her face, her eyes sparkling with excitement. "I love that you get to just call up *Rick Rollingsworth* and talk to him like a regular person."

Her exuberance made him chuckle. "Rick *is* a regular person." He paused. "Well, that's not entirely true. He is strangely obsessed with doing internet searches on himself."

"I can't help but be amazed, though. Weird quirks aside, the man has an impressive body of work, and probably enough Oscars and Golden Globes to fill an entire trophy cabinet."

"That's why I called on him for help with this. Rick's

a good friend, and something of a mentor to me in the business." He drained the last of his root beer.

"If anyone can help you, I'm pretty sure he's got the connections you need." She turned her head to gaze out the window. "Promise me you'll go after what you want, Devon."

"I will." He watched her, taking in the regal beauty of her profile. She seemed to be admiring the scenery outside, and the enjoyment of that played over her features. She wore her emotions all over her face, and he knew from that moment that he'd do just about anything to make sure she was always happy.

Without taking her eyes off the window, she said, "I know you usually like to spend Christmas in quiet reflection and all, but…"

His brow cocked up. "But what?"

"My mother asked me to invite you to our house for Christmas dinner."

He hesitated.

She turned his way, her gaze dropping to the table. "Sorry. I just realized how that must have sounded." Her dark eyes lifted, and she looked right at him. "I would love it if you'd join us for Christmas dinner."

"Thank you for the invite." He had every intention of accepting, but he wanted to tease her a bit more.

"I have to warn you, the Monroes are big on Christmas. You can expect a huge tree, gaudy decorations, colored lights, gift exchanges…the whole nine yards." She smiled nervously. "I know you're not really into all that, but I'd appreciate it if you came."

"Will there be mistletoe?" He fixed her with a sly look, as if it weren't obvious why he'd posed the question.

She blushed. "Yes. Typically, no one makes use of it except Mom and Dad…"

"We'll just have to remedy that, won't we?" He winked.

The blush coloring her cheeks deepened in response, and she looked away.

"Don't get shy on me now, Hadley. We're in this thing, for real."

The waiter appeared then. As if he sensed he might be intruding, he quietly placed the bill on the table and slipped away.

Devon picked up the black leather folio, tucking a fifty-dollar bill inside. The amount covered both their meals, as well as a generous tip for their server. Then he stood, rounding the table, and offered his hand to help Hadley up from her seat. "Are you ready, baby?"

He'd thought her cheeks couldn't get any redder. But somehow they did as she accepted his hand. "Sure." Once she was on her feet, she slung her purse strap over her shoulder.

With a gentle tug, he pulled her into his embrace. "You seem a little nervous about the whole mistletoe thing. So, let's practice."

And before she could utter another word, he pressed his lips to hers. She was a little stiff at first, as if the kiss caught her off guard. Within seconds, she relaxed, draping her graceful arms around his shoulders.

He kissed her long and deep, ignoring the few other

people in the restaurant. And when he released her, breaking the seal of their lips, she sighed softly.

Pleased that he could get her to make that sound, he smiled and escorted her out of the restaurant.

# Chapter 9

Hadley entered the family room at her parents' house quietly that evening. She'd come straight there after leaving the office, hoping to act on Devon's advice about going over her brothers' heads. In any other instance, she might have waited awhile and taken a shot at reasoning with Savion, but with so much at stake, she didn't want to risk wasting valuable time.

Monroe Manor, as the family referred to the house, was a two-story brick-and-stone structure occupying a five-acre lot on the northeastern side of the island. Her childhood home was roomy, over three thousand square feet, with six bedrooms and three and a half baths. The verdant green lawn behind the house went on for several hundred yards before it gave way to a broad strip of sand, then to the cerulean waters of the

Atlantic. It wasn't the largest home on the island, but it was in the top five.

She'd used her key to get inside and shut the door behind her. There was no telling what her parents would be up to this time of the day, but she knew they were home. She'd passed through the three-car garage and entered through the kitchen, and noticed both cars and both motorcycles were parked inside.

The family room was Hadley's favorite room in the house. The crisp white walls, along with the soft shades of blue, green and tan her mother had chosen for the furniture and decor, were a perfect reflection of the coastline outside. The picture window behind the beige sofa allowed plenty of light to shine in. Making herself comfortable on the couch among her mother's bevy of throw pillows, Hadley looked outside at the grassy expanse that led to the road. She loved looking out the window at the pristine scenery of the other homes and landscaped lawns nearby, so she thought she'd watch before she combed the house in search of her parents.

She didn't have to go looking, because her mother strolled into the family room, carrying a magazine and a cup of hot tea. At fifty-six, Viola Monroe still possessed the appearance of someone fifteen years her junior. She wore a pair of white palazzo pants and a white T-shirt and had her gray-streaked curls, as well as her reading glasses, piled on top of her head. She looked up from the magazine as she sensed her daughter's presence. "Hello, sweetheart. What are you doing here in the middle of the week?"

"Hi, Mom." Climbing up from the couch, Hadley

went over to give her mother a kiss on the cheek. "I was hoping to talk to you and Daddy."

Viola's brow furrowed as she set her teacup and magazine on the side table. "It must be important for you to come over out of the blue. Your father's in his study, flipping through that stamp book again."

Hadley sighed. Tugging her father's attention away from his prized stamp collection would be a challenge. "I'm going back there."

Settling into her favorite armchair, Viola cracked, "Good luck, dear."

Hadley walked through the foyer, past the staircase and into the rear hallway. There, she knocked on the solid oak door of her father's study. "Dad? Can I come in?"

A few seconds later he answered, "Sure, Hadley."

She pressed down on the gold handle and opened the door. Peering into the room, with its pine wainscoting, flooring and bookcases, she saw her dad in the center of it all.

Carver sat behind his big pine desk, leaning forward. She could see the light from his desk lamp reflecting off the top of his head, which was sparsely covered by his thinning, close-trimmed gray hair. He clutched a magnifying glass in his hand as he pored over the open pages of the stock book holding his stamps. Without looking up, he said, "Hi, honey. What are you doing here in the middle of the week?"

She chuckled, releasing some of her nervous energy. "Mom just asked me the same thing. I was hoping to talk to you and Mom about something."

"Okay." He flipped the page, closely studying the contents.

She watched him for a few minutes. When she realized he'd fallen back down the stamp rabbit hole, she spoke again. "Daddy, could you come in the family room with us, please? It will just take a few minutes, then you can get back to what you're doing."

"Sounds reasonable." He set his magnifying glass aside and closed the book, following her to the front of the house.

Once they were all comfortably seated in the family room, Hadley and Carver on the sofa and Viola ensconced in the overstuffed armchair across from them, Hadley squared her shoulders.

Taking a deep breath, she started talking. "I'm here because I think Savion is about to make a bad business decision, and I'd like to prevent that, if possible."

Carver's brow cocked. "What bad business decision?"

"Do you know about the Neville South offer on our land?"

He nodded. "Of course I do. But what does that have to do with anything?"

Hadley frowned. "Everything. Daddy, Neville South doesn't care about the people in Sapphire Shores or creating jobs or any of that. They're just out to make a buck, while pushing out the people who already own businesses here on the island."

He chuckled. "There's that youthful idealism of yours."

She wasn't amused, especially since his tone and

his expression were basically the equivalent of patting her on the head. "It's more than that, Daddy. Bringing all those chain stores to the island is going to ruin the unique charm we have here. And why can't they make room for local businesses, anyway? Della already told me she wants to expand, and I—"

Carver sighed, placing a hand on his daughter's shoulder. "Hadley, calm down. No one has signed anything yet. But I'm going to be honest with you. I agree with your brother. It's a good offer, and it could bring a lot of good things to the island, too."

Resisting the urge to roll her eyes, she turned away. "You sound just like him. I'm sure you're thinking of the money right now, aren't you?"

"I'd be lying if I said I wasn't." Carver shrugged, his arms moving beneath the fabric of his pajama top. "Did you know that they're offering two and half times what the land is worth? I don't see accepting that as a bad business decision."

"Daddy, you're not listening."

He patted her shoulder. "I've heard everything you said, honey. I just disagree."

She swiveled toward Viola. "Mom. Please jump in here and tell Dad…"

"Oh, no, you don't." Viola waved a hand from behind the pages of her magazine. "I'm not about to step into that minefield."

"Mom, I just think…"

"This is precisely why I retired. After almost forty years taking care of this family, plus helping to run the business, I'm tired."

Hadley stared at her mother, amazed. "Come on, Mom. You must have an opinion on this. I know you do."

"I sure do. And I'm keeping it right to myself." She raised the magazine a little higher, turning the page as she lapsed back into silence.

Letting her head drop back against the cushions of the sofa, Hadley sighed. She wasn't going to get anywhere with her parents on this issue. If she was going to stop the Neville South deal, she'd have to do it herself.

Devon strolled out onto the patio Thursday afternoon with his tablet in hand. He wanted to do a little online shopping with the local grocery store, Shoreside Foods. The locally owned market had embraced the rise of technology and leveraged it for the convenience of their customers. Because of that, they now had a delivery service, so customers could shop online and have their items delivered to their door. The service had been implemented since Devon's last visit, and now that he'd discovered it, he was quite pleased. He needed to replenish a few things he'd used up since his arrival—milk, eggs and the like. He also planned to order some fresh flowers and a few surprises for Hadley.

Seated on the resin love seat, he started perusing Shoreside Foods' website. The day was partly cloudy, with mild temperatures and a cool breeze blowing from the Atlantic. In his gray sweats and sneakers, he was comfortable and warm despite the crisp air. The quietness, broken only by the soothing sound of the waves, helped to still his mind. This was why he chose to spend his holiday vacation here, in his hometown. No other place on Earth had ever seemed so peaceful and so antithetical to the pace and tone of life in Los Angeles.

A notification on an incoming video call filled the screen, blocking his view of the store's website. Seeing the name on the display, Devon smiled as he swiped the screen. "What up, Rick?"

"Hey, youngster." Rick's grinning face appeared on the screen. He gestured behind him, indicating that he was on foot and walking outdoors. "Look at this. Finally got away from the set and out to the ranch."

"I bet the wife and daughter are happy about that. Where are they?"

"Up at the house. I'm just out for some fresh air." He huffed a few breaths, as if taking on hilly terrain. "Whew. Anyway, I've got some news on the Panther project."

Devon's face brightened. "Great. Let me hear it."

"Well, first off, the movie's got a title now. *Love in the Revolution.*"

"Nice." He was eager to hear what else Rick might have for him, so he encouraged him. "Go on."

"The other news is that I was able to pull some strings for you and snag you a role." The moving scenery stopped as Rick dropped down onto a bench somewhere on his property.

Devon's chest tightened as his excitement rose, but he kept it low-key. "Great, sounds great. So, when will I meet the screenwriter? Get a look at the script and all that?"

Rick's face crunched into a frown. "When we start

prepping for filming in February. Your agent will get all the details ironed out. Since when have you wanted to do all that before a role?"

*Hell, now I'm confused.* Frowning, Devon asked, "Okay, let's back up here. What role are you talking about?"

"They offered you the role of Stokely Carmichael, which I think is pretty damn good considering this isn't an action flick. Stokely played a big part in the party back then. It's an honor, really. I'm playing Bobby Seale."

He felt his frown deepen. "Rick, I thought I was clear when I said I was looking for a directing job, not an on-screen role."

Scoffing, Rick said, "You were clear. And I thought you were clearly joking."

He met that remark with silence, letting his expression speak for him.

Rick's face changed then, to a display of disbelief. "You mean you were serious?"

"Yes, I was."

Shaking his head, Rick replied, "So are you turning down the role? Because they already have a director."

Blowing out a breath, Devon nodded. "Yes, I'm turning down the role. I think it's a great concept, but I'm not looking for any more on-screen roles right now."

Rick shrugged. "All right, I'll let them know. But let me give you a little advice. You know, as a friend."

Devon braced for a real gem. "Sure. What is it?"

"Nobody here is going to take you seriously about this directing thing, Devon. You've been in the game almost ten years now, and you've never done anything but action and stunt work. That isn't gonna translate to you sitting in the director's chair."

He sighed. "That may be so, but it doesn't change what I want. I plan to find the right project and start my new career in directing."

Rick shook his head again, as if pitying Devon. "Do you, man, but don't expect any help from me. Later." And just like that, he disconnected the call.

Devon stood, tossing the tablet on the cushion. Frustration coursed through him like hot lava. Stripping off his sweatshirt, he stepped away from the love seat. If he were able to do so, he'd get in his car and head for the gym to take out his feelings on the heavy bag.

Yet his body had betrayed him, all because of the work he'd done—the work he was trying to leave behind. He looked back on his efforts over the years. After seventeen films, millions made at the box office, tons of fan mail and a beautiful home in one of the swankiest neighborhoods in Los Angeles, he wondered if it had all been worth it. Acting had taken him so many places and provided him with so many relationships and experiences. Still, how much did any of those things matter if he didn't have his health?

And as for those relationships he'd developed with his colleagues in the film industry, he wondered what they amounted to, as well. He'd considered Rick Rollingsworth, the Oscar- and Golden Globe–winning actor, to be one of his close friends. When he'd first come to Hollywood, he'd looked up to Rick. They'd worked together on half a dozen films, gone to countless red carpets and after-parties together. Devon had even spent time with Rick's wife and daughter. Yet none of that had meant a damn when it came time for Rick to help Devon achieve his innermost dream. Nothing in their past had stopped Rick from laughing in Devon's face when he'd shared his career hopes.

Pushing those thoughts away, he widened his stance. With his bare feet planted hip-width apart on the cool stone of the patio, he stretched, careful not to put too much stress on the muscles around his damaged disk. With his bare arms stretched up toward the sky, he took a series of deep breaths, focusing on the waves until he felt centered again.

With his peace restored, he grabbed his tablet and headed inside. Leaving the device on the coffee table, he retrieved clean linen from the closet in the hallway.

Later, under the hot spray of water flowing from the waterfall showerhead, he let his mind drift to more pleasant things—namely, Hadley. He hadn't called her today because he knew she was busy with end-of-the-year duties at work. That didn't preclude him from thinking of her, though. As he soaped his body, he recalled the way her lips felt pressed against his, the way she'd moaned when he'd darted his tongue over them.

His line of thinking soon began to affect his anatomy, so he tucked his fantasies away for later.

He would see her soon, and then perhaps his fantasies of her would become reality.

## Chapter 10

Hadley was both pleased and anxious to go over to Devon's place Friday for dinner. He hadn't given any indication that he'd tired of her cooking yet, and the thought made her smile. Now as she stood on the front porch of his town house, she smoothed her hands over the fabric of her cream-colored A-line skirt. She'd paired the skirt with a V-neck crimson top and under-stated gold jewelry and left her shoulder-length curls to hang down around her face.

She'd been standing there for a few moments but hadn't knocked yet. First, she needed to get her mind right. While her attraction to Devon was a long-standing part of her life, their relationship was still new. Logic told her she should take things slow and easy with him, but her body wanted the fast track. He'd mentioned not wanting to take the shortcut route with their relationship, and she'd agreed. Now she wondered if taking it slow would mean quelling the powerful physical desire that hung between them.

Drawing a deep breath, she knocked on the door.

He opened it, greeting her with a bone-melting smile. He wore a pair of well-fitting black jeans and a vintage Free Huey T-shirt. "Hadley. Come on in." He stepped aside to allow her entry.

She stepped out of the cool air and into the warmth of the town house, and he shut the door behind her. Before she could reach the sofa, he walked up behind her. His presence in her personal space threatened to overwhelm her.

He leaned into the crook of her neck and inhaled. "You smell wonderful."

With the fragrance of his cologne invading her senses and his muscular arms snaking around her waist, she barely managed a reply. "Thanks. So do you."

He placed a soft kiss against her throat before releasing her. "Let's sit down for a minute and talk." He moved to the window seat and patted the cushion next to him.

She eased onto the seat, close enough that their thighs touched.

He draped his arm around her lower back. "What would you like to make tonight?"

She shrugged. "I thought I'd make a nice pasta Bolognese. How does that sound?"

"Sounds great. Do I have all the things you need?"

She nodded. "Yes. I checked the refrigerator when I was here last time, so we're good."

He gave her a squeeze. "A man could get used to this, you know."

"Get used to what?" Being this close to him made it difficult to think critically. She'd come over to cook for him, and at this point it would be a miracle if she could remember the recipe. All she wanted to do was fall into his arms and have him carry her to the bed. The direction of her thoughts, coupled with the touch of her handsome companion, made her blush. *I have got to get it together.*

"Having a beautiful woman who's intelligent and loves to cook…" He paused, his gaze settling on her lips. "And kisses oh-so well."

A small sigh escaped her throat.

Seconds later, he pressed his lips to hers.

His kiss was gentle, yet held a fiery passion. His tongue darted along her lower lip, teasing and coaxing her to open her mouth. She did and was treated to the best, most intense kiss of her life. Their tongues mated, and she sank into his embrace as if she was made to be in his arms; that was how she felt.

A few breathless moments later, she eased away from him, a difficult but necessary action. Once she got her breath, she said, "If you want dinner, we're going to have to postpone the kissing until *after* I cook."

He chuckled as he put some distance between them. "I think you're right. If we keep this up…" He didn't finish his statement, but his eyes implied the rest.

She scooted off the window seat and scurried into

the kitchen. There she assembled everything she'd need for her Bolognese sauce on the countertop. To keep the sauce hearty while cutting cholesterol, she was using ground turkey instead of beef or pork. She'd also set out a large can of crushed plum tomatoes, white wine, chicken stock, minced garlic and various seasonings. Once she got the sauce simmering and the pasta boiling, she went to the sink to rinse her hands. As she dried them, she hazarded a glance his way.

His eyes were waiting.

To break the tension, she asked, "Has anything new happened with your career change?"

It worked, because his expression changed immediately. "Yes, but nothing good. Turns out Rick thought I was joking about the favor I asked of him. Basically, he dismissed me."

She frowned, sympathetic to the betrayal she sensed he felt. "I'm sorry that happened."

He shrugged. "It's no big deal. I'm going to put out some feelers elsewhere, see what I can come up with. Thankfully he's not the only person I know in Hollywood."

She returned to the stove, using a wooden spoon to stir the sauce. "You've got a good attitude about it. I'm sure things are going to work out eventually."

"What about you?" He shifted a bit, raising his legs up to rest his feet on the window seat's cushion. "How are things going with the developer's deal?"

The relative quiet of the space allowed her to hear him clearly. "We haven't made any official moves at the office yet." She lowered the burner temperature to keep the sauce from scorching. "But I did try talking to my parents the other night."

"And?"

She shook her head. "No luck there. Dad took Savion's side, per usual. And my mom is just too through with this kind of thing. She's vowed to keep her opinion on the matter to herself."

"Looks like we both struck out, huh?" He chuckled.

She shrugged. "Well, at least we live to fight another day. I don't intend to give up on my goals. Do you?"

His expression conveying his determination, he shook his head. "No way."

"Good." The pasta water bubbled up then, the foam threatening to spill over the rim of the pot. Slipping her hand into the oven mitt, she turned off the burner. Waiting a few seconds for the water to still, she then hauled the pot to the colander waiting in the sink and drained the contents.

As she worked on putting the pasta dish together, she could feel his eyes on her. Holding her awareness of him at bay for a moment, she scooped some of the sauce into a small bowl. Taking a spoon from the silverware drawer, she made her way to the window seat. There, she dipped the spoon into the sauce. "Want a taste?"

His brow hitched, as if he read the double meaning in her statement. "Yes. I definitely do."

She brought the spoonful of chunky red sauce to his lips.

He opened his mouth and tasted the sauce.

As she drew the spoon away, she asked, "How is it?"

"Delicious." His gaze met hers. "Almost as appealing as the chef."

Heat rushed into her cheeks. "Devon."

He grazed his knuckle over her cheek. "I meant exactly what I said." Then he snaked his right arm around her waist, drawing her close until she stood between his parted legs.

That damn tingling returned, buzzing through her body as the pace of her heartbeat increased. "I... I thought you didn't want to take shortcuts?" It seemed like the right thing to say, to remind him of what he'd said before.

"This isn't a shortcut. It's a natural progression." He nuzzled her neck.

She sighed, losing her grip on the spoon. It fell to the floor, and she couldn't muster an iota of concern.

He placed humid kisses against her throat, her collarbone and the shell of her ear. "If you want me to stop, Hadley, just say so."

She shivered. "Don't stop."

He lifted his head, looked into her eyes. "You're sure this is what you want?"

She nodded. "Yes."

"Then you'd better make sure the stove is turned off."

Once she'd done that, she returned to the window seat and climbed up.

Devon swept Hadley onto his lap as she scooted up on the window seat with him. Between them, his hardness pressed against her hip, making his longing for her clear. She settled in, a brief flicker of surprise passing over her face. Yet she gave no indication of being put off by his involuntary physical reaction to her.

Cradling her in his arms, he pushed a wayward curl out of the way with his fingertips. She trembled, and he wondered if she felt nervous now that the desire that had been bubbling between them had finally boiled over.

"Are you nervous?" He watched her face to gauge her reaction to the question.

She shook her head. "No. I feel safe with you."

Hearing that, he smiled. "Good. Because I would never hurt you." He slid his hands up to her shoulders, beginning to knead the tight muscles gently. He could feel the tension melting away beneath his touch as her back slumped against his chest.

She sighed. "That feels so good."

"Trust me. It gets better." He placed a soft kiss against the graceful line of her collarbone.

She hummed low in her throat.

He lifted his eyes to hers.

She swiveled to the side, her hands coming up to cup his jaw.

Moments later, his lips crushed against hers. Their bodies became a tangled mass as they embraced each other, his arms around her waist and her arms thrown around his neck. She opened to him right away, and his tongue explored the sweet, warm cavern of her mouth. She continued making the low humming sound, an indication of her enjoyment, against his lips.

When the kiss finally ended, their gazes met in the dim light. Only the light over the stove remained on, as full darkness had fallen outside. Yet even in the soft glow coming from the other room, he felt sure he read the wanting in her sparkling eyes.

What he saw didn't matter, not until she said yes. So, putting aside his own needs, he sought to draw out her true feelings.

He stroked her jaw, feeling the satin texture of her skin beneath his fingertips. "I didn't plan for this to happen so soon, Hadley."

She dropped her gaze. "Neither did I."

With crooked fingers, he tilted her chin so he could look into her beautiful eyes again. "I would never pressure you. But if you'll let me, I want to make love to you tonight."

She ran her index finger down the center of his chest. "Yes, Devon. Yes."

Needing no further encouragement, he stood. Once he was on his feet, he reached for her hand and tugged her up. Leading her by the hand, he walked through the living room, down the short hallway and into his bedroom.

Standing by the foot of the bed, he drew her into his arms. He didn't know how much experience she had with this, and in a way, it didn't matter. It was their first time together, and he fully intended to take things slow and give her all the pleasure she could stand.

Raking his hands through her loose curls, he kissed her lips again. Then he moved to her neck and the upper part of her chest, revealed by the V of her red top. She smelled of citrus and flowers, and he found the fragrance as soft and intoxicating as the woman wearing it.

He stepped back for a moment to peel off his T-shirt

and toss it aside. As he drew her back into his arms, she stroked her hands over his bare chest, fueling the fire already burning inside.

He kissed her again then, and the next few moments blurred into one another as he kissed and caressed her out of her top and the camisole she'd worn underneath.

With his arms still around her, he eased them both back toward the bed. Sitting down, he positioned her between his parted legs. He moved his hands to the side zipper on the waist of her long skirt. "Can I?"

With a wicked smile, she nodded.

He eased the zipper down, and she stepped out of the skirt. In nothing but a black lace bra and panties, she looked like an absolute goddess. The sight fired his blood even more.

He leaned forward, kissed the tops of her breasts where they rose above the bra. Her sighs were like music to his ears as he began to slip her out of the undergarments. As he undressed her, he kissed each new inch of bared skin. Her soft moans rose in the silence, and by the time she kicked her panties aside, her legs were shaking.

"Lie down," he instructed her quietly.

She did as he asked, and he stood to strip away his jeans and boxers.

Her gaze swept over his body, lingering on the hard evidence of his need. When she looked there, her lips tilted into a sensual smile. "Aren't you going to join me?"

"Soon." While he appreciated the invitation, his first mission was her ecstasy. With that in mind, he dropped to his knees at the end of the bed. His hands guided her hips to the edge of the mattress, and he nudged her thighs apart with his chin. She gasped as he placed a kiss on the inside of each thigh.

He lingered over her most intimate place then, bestowing her with the joy she deserved. Soft kisses gave way to lingering licks and impassioned sucks. With each gesture, her body arched, and her cries filled the bedroom. And as he gave her one slow, thorough lick, she shouted his name.

While she lay trembling on the bed, he stood. He gently readjusted her, moving her up toward the center of the bed. When she was properly positioned, he eased away to retrieve a condom. Sheathing himself with protection, he returned and moved on top of her, aligning his body with hers.

Before he could do anything else, she snaked her arms around his waist and pulled. Her action effectively brought their bodies together, and she purred as his hardness slipped inside her.

He had little time to settle into her insane tightness before instinct took over. He rocked his hips, stroking her with abandon. She met each stroke with one of her own, her hips rising off the bed.

They moved together as if their bodies had been made for oneness. He shifted, sliding his open palms down her sides and then beneath her. Filling his hands with her ample backside, he lifted her, angling her more to his liking. She squeaked out his name between fast, panting breaths. Then she lifted her legs and locked them around his waist. The new position allowed him to achieve deeper penetration, and he groaned with delight.

He watched her eyes close, then pop open again as the building sensations got the better of her. He struggled to keep a hold on his own pleasure, but as he watched her head drop back, he knew what was coming. She screamed, her body overtaken by waves of trembling as an orgasm carried her off.

And as he watched her climb to the highest heights, he followed her, growling as his own release propelled him heavenward.

# Chapter 11

Hadley opened her eyes to darkness and to the distinct feeling of not being in her own bed. As she blinked, letting her bleary eyes adjust to the low light, her mind began to awaken. She became aware of the strong arm tossed over her waist and the hard, naked body pressed against her back.

It didn't take long for realization to hit. The erotic memories of Devon's loving flooded her mind, bringing a smile to her face and a tingling warmth to the place between her thighs.

She shifted slowly, trying not to wake him. He groaned in his sleep, tightening his arm around her waist. The action caused her body to press closer to his, something she hadn't thought possible a few moments ago.

She felt his manhood awakening and stretching against her hip, and wondered why she'd wanted to get up in the first place.

She felt the movement as he tilted his head, then she felt his warm, soft lips lacing kisses along the side of her neck.

"Were you going somewhere?" His deep voice, thick with sleep and unmasked desire, reverberated in the silence.

"No." Why would she, when getting up now would mean denying herself another taste of his delectable lovemaking? She wanted this, wanted to let her body's cravings guide her actions instead of following the rule of logic.

So, as his kisses lingered, traveling lower, she gave herself over to the bliss. When he rolled her over a few moments later, she fed on his kiss greedily, wanting everything he had to give.

Their tangled limbs were wrapped in the bedsheets, but she adjusted accordingly until she was atop him. Straddling his strong hips, she made sure there was nothing between them.

Desire pushed her on, urging her to sink and take him in, but his hand on her belly stayed her. "The condom." His whispered reminder made her stop and move aside so he could retrieve the protection. When he returned to the bed with it, she took it from his hand. Encouraging him to lie on his back again, she knelt next to him and rolled the condom on.

The moment he was covered, she climbed into the saddle again. And this time, she didn't waste a moment lowering herself onto him. As she settled in, her inner thighs flush with his pelvis, she remained still for a moment. She savored the feel of him stretching her, filling her so gloriously. Then she began to move her hips, enslaved by the enticing sensations.

She leaned forward, bringing her upper body over his. He growled, his hands reaching up to cup her breasts. When he began to thumb her nipples, she answered with a purr of her own.

He continued to caress her fevered skin as she quickened her pace. She moved as fast as her desire demanded, until the rising ecstasy became too much. The glow of completion started where their bodies connected, radiating out through her belly and into all her limbs until it touched the very tips of her fingers and toes. And when she exploded, shouting her orgasmic joy into the steady strength of his muscled shoulder, he followed her a short time later.

Breathless and trembling, she lay against his chest in the aftermath. A sheen of sweat was the only thing between them, and that was just the way she liked it.

He slipped his arms around her, nuzzling her neck. "You're amazing."

She smiled, even though she knew he couldn't see her face. "You're not so bad yourself."

A snort of laughter met that remark. "Oh, so I guess you're gonna act like you weren't just screaming my name."

She blushed. "No, I'm not. Ain't no denying that." She'd never had a lover like him, someone who seemed almost obsessed with her pleasure. No man had ever

made it so clear to her that he valued her sexual fulfill-
ment over his own. The feeling she got from that was
unlike anything she'd ever felt before.

Maybe things would change between them one day.
Maybe he'd become as selfish as the other guys she'd
been involved with. Whatever the case, she'd never forget the care he'd shown for her tonight, or the way he'd
pushed her to the absolute limits of passion.

Emotions were running high—she could feel it.
Lying against him like this felt so good and so right,
it almost frightened her. What did it mean to be so
wrapped up in a man, especially one who had an entire
life waiting for him three thousand miles away? One
night with him had already changed her world, altering
her in a way she didn't think could be undone. What if
he decided she wasn't enough, that she wasn't a suitable replacement for the glitz and glamour of life in
Los Angeles? What if he chose his thousands of ador-
ing fans over her?

She wanted to ask him these things, but she couldn't
work up the nerve. Besides, parts of her were afraid of
what his answer might be.

So she set the questions aside for now, choosing instead to focus on the happiness she felt in the moment.
She'd finally made love to Devon after years of barely
contained attraction, and that warranted celebration.
Best of all, his loving had been better than any fantasy
she'd ever conjured up, and well worth the wait.

She wanted to say something, to tell him how wonderful a lover he'd been. But before she could get the words out, she heard his snores ruffling the silence.

With a sigh, she closed her eyes and let sleep claim her, as well.

Devon could have lain in bed forever with Hadley asleep in his arms. But morning eventually came, as it always did. And when the sun rose into the steel-blue sky, his eyes opened to the new day—and the new reality of the rapid progression of their relationship.

They'd shifted positions during the wee hours, and she now lay next to him, with her side resting atop his outstretched arm. Her wild curls lay spread across his pillow, highlighted by the golden rays of sunlight streaming through between the slats of the bedroom's vertical blinds.

He could feel the smile tilting his lips. There she lay, asleep and unadorned, and she was likely the most beautiful thing he'd ever laid eyes on. Fueled by his rising admiration, he leaned over and placed a gentle kiss against the warmth of her cheek.

She smiled first, then slowly opened her eyes. "Good morning."

"Morning." He pushed a few curls away from her face. "Sleep well?"

"The sleep I got was good, yes." She looked at him pointedly.

"I'm not sorry for keeping you up."

"And you shouldn't be. I'm not sorry about it." She lifted her face, puckering her lips.

Seeing no reason to deny her request, he kissed her,

slow and sweet. When he broke the seal of their lips, he said, "I'm guessing it's pasta Bolognese for breakfast?"

She laughed, nodded. "Yes. I'm not about to cook again, or let my made-from-scratch Italian feast go to waste."

He crawled out of bed then, extending his hand to her once he was on his feet. "Fair enough. But first, a shower." He didn't bother to hide the wicked glint in his eyes. She went along despite it…or maybe because of it.

He told himself they would simply shower and get out, because he didn't want to hold her captive all day. But as he stood beneath the stream of hot water, her lush, soapy nakedness so close to him, the idea of simply showering went out the window like a bird escaping its cage.

He pulled her body close to his, and she leaned forward, bracing herself with her palms against the shower wall. The sight of her positioned that way in the steamy stall threatened to make him spill then and there. That reminded him of the lack of protection and helped him quell his desire long enough for them to finish showering, get dressed and return to the kitchen.

At the dining room table, they enjoyed the meal that was supposed to have been their dinner the night before. The pasta was tender and the sauce flavorful with just a hint of spice. The similarities between the meal and its beautiful chef could not be denied.

As morning waned into afternoon, he stood by the door, giving Hadley a lingering kiss. She smiled up at him when they separated. "I have to go. I have something important I want to take care of today. But I'll call you, okay?"

He nodded, despite his selfish reluctance to let her go. No matter how much he wanted to hide her away and keep her all to himself, she had a life outside him, and he respected her enough to let her go about it. "Have a good day, baby."

With a blush reddening her cheeks, she wiggled her crimson-tipped fingers at him and left. He watched her climb into her car and drive away. Then he slipped back inside the town house and shut the door against the cool air.

Alone again, he settled down on the window seat with his phone and tablet. Turning sideways on the cushion, he stretched his legs out in front of him. The first doctor he'd seen after his injury had instructed him to put his feet up whenever he could, to take some of the stress off his lower back. He knew he could rest his feet on the coffee table, especially considering the rates he paid to rent this place. But when he was growing up, his mother had always forbidden him from putting his feet on her wooden furniture. Even though he was well into adulthood now, old habits died hard. The window seat was the perfect width to allow him to put his feet up while resting his back against its inner wall.

He opened the blinds, allowing the bright sunlight to provide light and warmth to his comfortable sitting spot. Picking up his phone, he put in a few calls to some of his friends and acquaintances on the left coast.

First, he called Corey Drake, his agent. Corey, who, at forty-three, had been in the game for more than a decade, was barely able to suppress his laughter as Devon spoke of his desire to try his hand at directing.

"Corey, remember, this is a partnership. So I'm going to need you to contain your amusement and put out some feelers for me, okay?"

"I get it, Dev." Corey sounded as if he were someplace crowded and shouted a bit to be heard over the noise around him. "I'll look into it."

"Good. Because the last thing I need is an agent who doesn't take me seriously." He hung up the phone then, before he was tempted to use a few choice words to tell Corey about himself.

The next call was to Glenn O'Hara, a set designer he'd met while filming the original *Destruction Derby* movie. Glenn was a little more respectful of Devon's request, though he seemed somewhat unsure of how he could help.

"What do you need me to do, Mr. Granger?"

Devon chuckled. "First, call me Devon. I'm asking you to keep your ear to the ground. I'm serious about moving out of acting and into directing, and you've got relationships with plenty of producers and screenwriters."

"That's true." Glenn seemed to be turning the request over in his mind. "I'll see what I can do, Mister… I mean Devon. Sorry about that. Most actors at your level don't go for being called by their first names."

"You and a whole lot of other folks are about to find out just how different I am from *other* actors. Thanks for your help, Glenn."

"No problem." And he ended the call.

Devon set the phone aside for a moment. He didn't know what or how much Glenn would be able to do for him. But the man had been receptive, so Devon placed the call firmly in the win column.

He didn't expect anyone to give him special treatment or to go out of their way to lay rose petals at his feet. All he asked was that people not lay traps and obstacles along the new path he was trying to take. His college coursework had yielded him a dual degree in drama and film; he'd done a short film on systemic racism for his senior project. He knew he had the skill to sit in the director's chair, and he intended to put it to use. That was why he was still angry with Rick Rollingsworth. Rick's callous dismissal of Devon's aspirations had been a hard blow. But at least Rick had shown his true colors, so Devon would know not to expect much from him in the future. He did, however, vow to rub his directorial success in Rick's face the very moment he made it.

After a quick break to grab a glass of iced tea and a bowl of popcorn, Devon returned to the window seat and to his task. He used the tablet to fire off a few emails to people he was acquainted with but unable to reach by phone. He kept his messages short and succinct, mindful of the abject busyness that plagued most folks in the industry, and of his own annoyance at getting long-winded emails. Once he'd finished that, he set the tablet down on the window seat and relaxed against the wall behind him.

As the sweet tea rushed in a cool torrent down his throat, he thought back on the previous night. He imagined that from now on, whenever he didn't have something pressing on his mind, his thoughts would always return to Hadley. In the few days since she'd been his girlfriend, she'd already left an unmistakable imprint on his world. And now that they'd made love, the connection between them had only deepened.

He looked out the window at the overcast day. Even though he knew he needed his rest, he craved some fresh air. So, donning his sneakers, he tucked his phone into the hip pocket of his track pants, slipped on a jacket and left the house to take a short walk.

As he locked the door, a thought made him smile.

*If I'm going to have a woman like Hadley in my life, I'd better keep my blood pumping.*

## Chapter 12

After she swung by her house for a change of clothes, Hadley went out with a single mission in mind: proving to her brothers that the offer from Neville South wasn't good for Sapphire Shores. In her mind, the best way to do that was to ask the citizens. After all, the island was their home, and they deserved to have a say in the matter.

Anticipating that she'd spend most of the afternoon on her feet, she'd dressed casually in a pair of white jeans, a dark blue sweater and blue-and-white sneakers. Tucking her hair up into a haphazard bun, she grabbed her supplies. Filling a canvas beach bag with two clipboards holding printed copies of her petition, and about thirty ballpoint pens, she left the house and headed for downtown.

Before she left work Friday, she'd spent time at her desk, working out her plan. She'd made a list of business owners in town she wanted to approach, as well as places frequented by everyday citizens of the island. Then, she'd written up a simple petition with spaces to collect signatures. Her main goal wasn't necessarily to convince people to sign the petition, though that would further her cause. She really just wanted to hear from the people of Sapphire Shores. Unlike her brothers, she cared about their opinion. And if the overwhelming majority of them wanted to let the developer go ahead with construction, Hadley would be willing to lay down her weapons. She wasn't one to fight a needless battle.

When she parked in the main lot near the intersection of Fable Drive and Story Road, she got out with the bag slung over her shoulder. Her first stop was an easy and familiar one. Wearing a smile, she pushed open the doors to Crowned by Curls and went inside.

The salon was just as crowded as it was on most Saturday afternoons. The interior bustled with activity and conversation, from the filled chairs in the waiting area to the reception desk and the styling floor behind the beaded curtains. Seeing Sandra standing at the desk talking to Lisa, Hadley made her way over.

"Hey, Sandra. Hey, Lisa." She touched Sandra's arm. "Can I talk to you for a minute?"

"Sure, girl." Sandra gestured for Hadley to follow her, then passed through the beaded curtain and across the styling floor, leading Hadley into her office in the back of the building. She sat at her desk and gestured for Hadley to sit across from her.

"This won't take long, because I know y'all are busy today."

Sandra shrugged. "It's cool. I don't have another client for an hour or so. What's up?"

Settling into her seat, Hadley spent a few minutes explaining the Neville South offer. When she finished, she asked, "What's your opinion on this?"

Sandra's brow furrowed. "So, you're telling me this developer is dead set against having local businesses in the new shopping area they want to open?"

She nodded. "Yes. They plan to fill most of the storefronts with chains and franchises, and the few that are left may be open, but only to new small businesses. Existing small businesses won't be eligible to lease space there, at least not at the rates they'll be charging." Even as Hadley explained the proposal, she shook her head. For the life of her, she couldn't understand the developer's seemingly malicious intent to squash the island's economy.

Sandra rolled her eyes. "Do they think that if they keep us out of their saditty development, we'll be forced out of business? Because Crowned by Curls is making good money, and we aren't going anywhere."

"I know. And I can't help being worried about the other businesses that are established here but aren't as quite as successful as you are." She didn't mention them aloud, but she thought of Della's, the Shoreside Foods and all the small boutiques selling handmade jewelry, stationery and things that represented hours of creative labor.

Sandra snorted. "You're right. Maybe they think they

can force us out and take control of the island's whole economy."

Hadley's eyes widened. "That's it, Sandra. All this time, Savion has been ignoring me when I said the developer was motivated by greed. But I've had this horrible feeling about Neville South, and you just articulated why." She leaned back, tenting her fingers. "I can't imagine he'll keep ignoring my warnings when I point this out to him."

"I hope you're right." Sandra sighed, her expression still communicating her anger at what she'd heard. "Listen, is there anything I can do to help you stop this from happening?"

With a smile, Hadley took a clipboard and pen out of her bag. "There sure is. Sign this petition."

Sandra scribbled her signature in the first open space. "And I think once we talk to our clients, they'll all want to sign it, too. At least the locals. I'm not sure how concerned the tourists will be." She passed the clipboard and pen back.

Hadley accepted the items and stood. "That's fine. I'm really looking to show my brothers the will of the island's full-time citizens, anyway. So it's all right if the tourists don't want to sign."

"Cool. Come on up front and I'll let you use the PA system."

Sandra went around the styling floor, asking all the stylists to turn off the all the dryers, both handheld and hooded, so everyone could hear Hadley's announcement. Using the handset of the desk phone, Hadley gave an honest account of the developer's offer to the patrons in the salon. She kept it brief but detailed and ended by asking that anyone interested in signing the petition against the new development report to the desk.

By the time she set both clipboards and her stash of pens on the counter, a line had already started to form. Apparently, the women of Sapphire Shores didn't appreciate the blatant profiteering Neville South sought to engage in at their expense. Hadley watched woman after woman—most of them draped in styling capes and sporting curlers, conditioning caps or coloring foils— sign the petition. It gratified her to know that so many of her fellow citizens were of a similar mind as her.

When she left with her clipboards, she'd collected twenty-six signatures from the patrons and staff of the salon. Outside, she started down the sidewalk. A few doors down from the salon, she stopped by the bakery and spoke with the proprietor there. It wasn't as crowded as the salon, but she collected seven more signatures, which accounted for all but one of the people inside the establishment.

She traveled on foot as far as she could, visiting four more businesses to collect signatures. Then she climbed back into her car, having collected fifty-seven signatures total during her time downtown. Starting the engine, she set off for Della's.

The deli was much quieter than during the weekday lunch rush, but was still mostly full. Hadley spent time talking to Ralph, Della's husband, who worked on Saturdays so his wife could have some time at home. Their conversation led to Ralph's signature on the petition, and Hadley left with a sandwich and thirteen additional signatures on her petition sheets.

As the afternoon faded into evening, Hadley visited several more businesses, and then drove home. Inside the house, she laid her petition sheets out on the table and counted the signatures she'd collected. Altogether, she'd managed to get 217 people to sign. Since Sapphire Shores had a year-round population of fewer than seventy-five hundred people, she considered that an impressive number, especially since she'd collected them all in a single day. Tucking the signed pages into a folder, she left it on the table.

She thought of all the people she'd spoken to today, and those she hadn't. Whether she talked to them, and regardless of if they had agreed with her or not, many of them would be adversely affected if the developer's proposal was accepted.

She looked at the bright red folder holding the petition and smiled.

When the time came to defend her hometown and theirs, she'd be ready.

Devon strolled along the beach Saturday evening, enjoying the feel of his bare feet sinking into the cool sand. What he enjoyed more was having Hadley walking next to him, her small hand in his. The darkened sky above sparkled with stars and the faint light of a crescent moon. The tableau was beautiful but came in close second to his companion.

She'd changed after she left that morning and now wore a pair of jeans and a sweater. When he'd invited her to walk on the beach, he hadn't been sure she'd go for it. But she'd accepted right away, though she'd refused to take off her shoes, preferring to keep her feet out of the sand due to the coolness hanging in the air.

"So, what did you do today? If you don't mind my asking."

"Remember how I didn't have any luck with my parents about this Neville South thing?"

"Yes, I remember."

"Well, today I went into town and collected signatures on a petition against the developer's proposal."

He nodded, impressed with both her efforts and her determination to take on one of the largest developers in the Southeast. "Wow, Hadley. That's a brilliant idea. How many signatures did you get?"

"Over two hundred." She smiled, looking proud of her accomplishment. "It's more than enough to keep Savion from ignoring my concerns this time."

"I agree." He knew the island wasn't big enough to support a very large year-round population, so the signatures she'd gotten represented a good cross section of them. "I'm really impressed that you came up with this and that you were able to execute it so quickly."

She asked, "What about you? Any progress on your career move?"

He could only shrug. "I'm not sure yet. I did put in some calls and send emails to a few contacts. I'm hoping at least one of them will come through for me."

"That's good. At least you're still trying." She squeezed his hand.

"Yep. And I fully intend to keep at it until I make

this move." He looked up at the sky, observing the rising darkness. "It's time."

"You know I'm behind you. Whatever it is you're after, I'm sure you can do it." She moved a little closer to him as they kept walking.

He released her hand so he could drape his arm around her shoulder. Having her close to him made him feel as if he could accomplish anything, even his so-called crazy dream of becoming a director.

She stopped suddenly, moving closer to the water and casting her gaze up to the sky. "Look at that. Isn't it gorgeous?"

"Yes, it is." His response was as much about her as the sky. He looked to the heavens, taking in the deep richness of the night sky, punctuated by gleaming silver stars. She stood on her tiptoes, raising her face toward his.

He leaned down and kissed her on the lips. His arms circled her shapely body, pulling her flush against him. Her lips were pliant and soft, and when he swept his tongue over the petal of her lower lip, she opened to him without hesitation.

He could go on kissing her for hours, but after several long, torrid moments, he released her.

She looked up at him, silently regarding him.

He watched her as well, lost in the shimmering beauty of her dark brown eyes.

Without thinking, he murmured the words that seemed to fit this moment, the words that his heart had kept locked away for so long.

"I love you, Hadley."

# Chapter 13

Hadley blinked a few times as her mind worked through what Devon had said. *Did he just say what I think he said?* After a few moments of confusion, she finally put her mouth in gear. "What did you say?"

His beautiful golden eyes locked on her face. "I said, I love you, Hadley."

Her heart fluttered in her chest, and tears sprang to her eyes. "Oh, my."

He met her exclamation with a soft chuckle. "That wasn't the response I expected."

She could only nod to convey her understanding. This relationship was still so new. But after all the time she'd spent fantasizing that he would say those words to her, it seemed like she'd been waiting an eternity to hear them.

"You don't have to say it back." His deep voice cut through her thoughts.

She looked up at him, searching his face. Was he angry? Hurt? Embarrassed? She didn't see any of those things. His expression exuded nothing but affection for her.

"I… I…" she stammered, searching for a way to express what she felt.

He smiled. "It's cool. I know you have feelings for me, or else you wouldn't have approached me."

She inhaled, filling her lungs slowly.

He placed gentle hands on her shaking shoulders. "Remember what I said. No shortcuts. No pressure."

A wave of emotion came over her, the force of it surpassing the ocean crashing against the shore. She leaned into him, craving him.

He caught her in his embrace and wordlessly turned, walking them toward the back patio of the town house.

He stooped to pick up the moccasins he'd kicked off by the back door, then left the patio door open after he escorted her inside.

He stopped at the dining room table. When he sat down at the head of it, she assumed he would pull her onto his lap.

Instead, he brought her to stand next to him. Then he ran his palms over the flat of her stomach before circling her hips. "You seem tense. Let me relax you, baby."

Trembling, she watched his hands move around to the front of her waist, where his fingers lingered at the button of her jeans.

"Can I?" He looked up for her answer.

"Yes…" Her answer came on the heels of a sigh. Swirling heat began to gather between her thighs as her body anticipated the things he would do to her.

So he undid her jeans, first the button, then the zipper. As he tugged them down her legs, she helped him along by wriggling out of them and then kicking them aside. Next, he helped her out of her sweater, leaving her in only her camisole, bra and panties.

He patted the table in front of him. "Have a seat."

She did as he asked, rising to rest her hips on the tabletop. He eased her thighs apart, then shifted until he pulled his chair up between them.

A shiver ran through her as his fingertips grazed over her skin, tracing a pattern from her ankles to the insides of her upper thighs.

"So sweet…" His murmured words accompanied his motions as he stroked his knuckle over her core, with only the thin satin of her panties between his hand and her sensitive flesh.

The touch hit her like a thunderbolt, as if there were no barrier between them. She fell back then, resting on her elbows to support her upper body.

He smoothly pushed the fabric aside, easing his hand into her panties. His touch was gentle, purposeful and skilled as he swept two fingers over her damp warmth.

Another wave of trembles took over her body as the bliss began to build. What was he doing to her? He seemed to have mystical power over her body, something that gave him the ability to send her beyond the limits of self-control.

Her head dropped back as he continued his ministrations, and when he tugged her panties away, she offered no protest. Then, with her legs spread and her very center bared to him atop his dining room table, he leaned in and kissed the place he'd been so skillfully stroking.

A strangled cry left her lips when she felt his first lick, and more cries and moans followed as he continued. Reality fell away; time became meaningless. All she cared about was Devon, his hands gripping her hips and his wicked mouth driving her out of her mind.

He kept up his attention, never wavering from his mission until she screamed into the silence of the room. Orgasm tossed her toward the stars, and as she came down, shaking and sighing, she knew no other man would ever compare to him.

When she got her bearings enough to move, she sat upright again. Seeing the wicked smile on his face, she said breathlessly, "You are too much."

He shook his head. "Nope. I'm exactly what you need."

She smiled. *He's certainly not lacking in charm.* "What I need right now is help off this table before you get any more ideas."

"I was just about to help you." He stuck out his hands.

She grabbed hold of them, only to be tugged down onto his lap.

"Does this suit you better, baby?" He held her close, watching for her response.

She shook her head, knowing she had little to no resistance when it came to him. "I think I can work with it."

\* \* \*

Late Sunday morning, Devon awakened in his bed alone. Hadley had gone home after their interlude in the dining room. She'd said exhaustion had taken hold, and they both knew if she stayed, no one would've gotten any sleep.

Climbing out of bed, he went about his usual morning routine. Refreshed from a shower, he sat down to a simple breakfast of cereal, toast and a banana.

As he walked across the room to the couch, intent on spending some time reading, he heard his phone ringing. Grabbing it from its spot on the coffee table, he answered it. "Hello?"

"Good morning, Mister... I mean, Devon."

Recognizing the voice on the other end, Devon smiled. "What's up, Glenn? I didn't expect to hear back from you so soon."

"I've spoken to several writers already, as well as a studio head I know." Glenn paused. "I already had a meeting scheduled at the studio, so I figured I'd go ahead and ask around."

"And what did you find out?"

Glenn's tone changed, becoming less upbeat. "It's not looking good. The studio head says you're crazy. Most of the writers laughed. I can't say I made much headway for you."

Devon sighed. When he'd realized Glenn was calling him back on a Sunday, he'd thought the news was good. "Tomorrow is Christmas Eve. This is a hell of a present."

"There is one positive, though. One of the writers—the one who didn't laugh—had a suggestion for you."

Devon rolled his eyes. This ought to be good. "And what was that?"

"Open a production company." Glenn paused, and took a deep breath. "Think about it. You have the industry experience to get it done, and if it's your company, no one will be able to stop you from directing, or doing anything else you want."

Flopping down on the couch, Devon touched his temple. "I don't know, Glenn. Going indie is a lot of work, and I'm not sure I'd be able to handle everything that entails."

"It's just a suggestion. I respect you, and I believe you can do well as a director." Glenn sighed. "If there's anything else I can do to help you, please reach out. But I think you've probably hit a dead end out here."

He sighed, knowing Glenn was probably right. Now that he'd reached out to so many people about this directing thing, the word was out. Odds were there were a bunch of studio types laughing at him all over Los Angeles. "All right. Thanks anyway, Glenn."

After he disconnected the call, Devon sat back against the sofa cushions. As he turned Glenn's secondhand suggestion over in his mind, he wondered if starting his own company was really his only solution. Running a business wasn't something he'd ever aspired to. All he really wanted to do was the creative, artistic work of bringing a writer's vision to life on screen. Now he was moving into territory he wasn't sure he wanted to explore.

Tossing the phone aside, he scratched his chin. He didn't want to think too hard about it now; after all, this was supposed to be his vacation. He turned his mind to Hadley and to the Monroe family Christmas dinner. He'd asked repeatedly if he could bring something and had been turned down each time. Hadley had warned him that the Monroes were big on Christmas, and that he could expect to find the atmosphere "overwhelmingly festive." He'd chuckled when she'd described it that way, but parts of him wondered if he could sit through it. He was honored to be invited, but he didn't have much interest in holiday movies, gift exchanges or dramatic readings of "A Visit from St. Nicholas."

In the end, he decided not to worry about it. All that really mattered was getting to spend the day with Hadley. And if that meant participating in her family's holiday jamboree, so be it.

If he was lucky, he'd be able to hold on to some of that holiday cheer to get him through the following day. December 26 would be the fifth anniversary of Natalie's death. Though time seemed to soften his pain, that day still usually felt dark and somber.

Setting aside his worries, he turned on the television. He flipped through the channels until he found some trashy reality show. Then he settled in to watch the train wreck, letting it take his mind off his troubles.

## Chapter 14

Christmas day was here, and as Hadley buzzed around the house that day helping her mother set up for dinner, she kept thoughts of Devon in the back of her mind.

Viola, dressed in her traditional Christmas outfit of a red sweater and emerald green skirt, tied an apron over her clothes. "Hadley, set the table for me. I'm going to start pulling out the things that need to be warmed up."

"Yes, ma'am." Hadley knew that was the only acceptable response to her mother's shouted instructions. Viola had never been particularly stern with her children, but when it came to her holiday dinners, Viola Monroe meant business.

As Hadley rolled the silver cart with the holiday china and table service on it into the dining room, she wondered what Devon was doing. It was midafternoon, and he was due to arrive within an hour or so. Thinking of him made heat rise into her cheeks as she recalled the naughty way he'd calmed her nerves a few days ago. It certainly wasn't something she should be thinking of while setting her mother's table, but she couldn't help it. The man was a champion lover, and keeping her mind on the straight and narrow when it came to him was very difficult.

She laid out the snow-white tablecloth, then set the table with dishes, stemware and silver, following the pattern her mother had taught her as a child. Being the only girl in the Monroe family had meant spending hours with her mother learning how to do traditional women's work: setting tables, cleaning, cooking and taking care of her appearance. Her father had balanced it out by taking her fishing and golfing. Hadley supposed all those things made her a well-rounded individual. Given the choice, though, she'd probably never go golfing again. The game had bored her so much she'd often nodded off sitting in her father's golf cart.

Once she'd finished setting the table, she pushed the silver cart back into the pantry and turned to her mother for more instructions.

Before Viola could open her mouth, the doorbell rang.

Hadley couldn't hold back her smile as she jogged past her mother, through the kitchen, into the foyer and to the front door to open it.

On the porch she found a smiling Devon. He looked delectable in a pair of black slacks, a tan sweater and tan-and-black dress shoes. A silver chain hung around his neck, and he had a velvet wine-bottle bag tucked under his arm. With a blinding smile, he greeted her. "Merry Christmas. You look beautiful, baby." He leaned in and pecked her on the cheek.

She knew he was prone to kissing her way more intensely than that but figured he was being respectful of her parents' house. "Thank you. And merry Christmas." She'd dressed as her mother's dinners demanded—a little black dress that barely grazed her knees, black pumps and a string of pearls. Eyeing the wine, she said, "You brought something."

He passed her the bag. "Yes. I know you said not to, but I appreciate the invite."

"I'll give it to Mom. Come on in." She stepped aside so he could enter, then retraced her steps toward the kitchen. She could feel Devon following close behind.

At the kitchen door, Viola greeted them. She'd taken off her apron and now held her arms up for their guest. "Devon. It's so good to see you."

Sharing an embrace with her, Devon smiled. "Good to see you, too, Mrs. Monroe."

"Oh, none of that. Call me Vi." Seeing the bag Hadley held, she took it. "Did you bring this? You know you didn't have to bring anything."

He chuckled. "I know. Hadley told me. But I thought you'd enjoy it. Merry Christmas."

"Aren't you sweet? Merry Christmas to you, too." Viola undid the strings, lifting the bottle from its bag. Her eyes widened as she looked at the label. "My word. Ten-year-old cabernet! Thank you, dear."

"You're welcome." He draped his arm around Hadley's shoulders. "Thank you for raising such a classy, wonderful daughter."

Hadley looked to her mother for a reaction. She hadn't really spoken to Viola about what was happening between her and Devon. Viola's grin told all, communicating her approval even better than words could have. "Well, look at you two. Come on in the family room and see the boys."

Hadley groaned inwardly. Ever since she could remember, her mother had referred to the men of the household collectively that way. She braced herself for whatever crazy reactions her father and brothers might have to her new boyfriend.

Carver, seated on the couch, looked up from the open book on his lap as they entered, and he smiled. "Devon Granger. Merry Christmas. Long time no see. How are you, son?"

"Merry Christmas. I'm good, Mr. Monroe. How about you?"

"Can't complain." The older man nodded, then his eyes moved lower, settling on Devon's hand, which was wrapped around Hadley's. His expression changed then, becoming less open and more questioning.

Hadley held her breath. She knew better than to read too much into her father's use of the endearment *son*—Carver frequently used the term when speaking to younger men. Truthfully, she had no idea what he would say next.

Carver started to speak. "Well, I—"

Before he could get his sentence off the ground,

Campbell entered the room, arms laden with wrapped gifts. "Merry Christmas, y'all."

As everyone in the room responded in kind, he set the gifts under the seven-foot Fraser fir occupying a corner of the room. "Savion is on his way in with the rest."

Hadley took the opportunity to sit down next to her father. His body language seemed a bit stiff, but he said nothing.

Devon sat down in one of the two armchairs.

Savion entered then, toting several gift bags, which he also placed beneath the tree. "Ho, ho, ho, folks."

Viola took the empty armchair, and Savion leaned against the back. Campbell took a seat on the carpet near the tree.

A few moments passed in silence before Carver asked, "Devon, what's going on between you and my little girl?"

Hadley fought the urge to roll her eyes. She was damn near thirty years old, and had long since grown tired of her parents referring to her that way.

Devon, on the other hand, appeared completely relaxed. "As of last week, we're dating. And you should know that I plan to treat her like the queen she is."

Warmth rushed to her cheeks in response to Devon's words.

Carver looked less impressed but said nothing more.

Savion inclined his head. "You'd better. We Monroe men are very protective of Mom and Hadley. I'd hate to have to kick your ass."

"Duly noted," Devon answered with a smile. If he

was at all intimidated by the Monroe men, he didn't let on. He remained just as cool while they continued to pepper him with questions, both about his intentions with Hadley and the latest happenings in his career.

Hadley felt some of the tension leave her body, and the room. Devon's ability to remain calm impressed her and added to his list of positive qualities.

When Viola called them to dinner, they sat around the table, and after Carver blessed the meal, they all dined on a sumptuous feast. Glazed ham, garlic mashed potatoes, roasted root vegetables, homemade rolls and more all made their rounds of the table. Conversation flowed easily, even as Savion and Carver attempted to intimidate Devon. He let their barbs roll of his back, answering with a smile.

After the plates were cleared away, Hadley grabbed Devon by the arms and secreted him away to the rear of the house. Just outside the back door, she draped her arms around his neck. "Look up."

His gaze lifted to the strategically placed sprig of mistletoe. "You put that there, didn't you?"

She winked. "You know the deal, Devon."

"Yes indeed." And he pulled her closer in his arms and kissed her until her knees went weak.

Devon pulled his rental car into the small parking lot of Mt. Ephraim Baptist Church and cut the engine. The day after Christmas had dawned cloudy and overcast, and those conditions continued to linger. Stepping out of the car, he closed his lightweight trench against the chill hanging in the air and hurried to the main doors of the church.

The redbrick church he'd attended with his parents as a child hadn't changed much since last year. But he did notice new brass door handles as he stepped up onto the cement pad in front of the entrance. For the past four years, he'd come here on December 26. He didn't consider himself especially religious and knew he certainly wasn't as pious as his mother would like. Still, coming here each year, on this day, helped him deal with his reality as a widower in a healthy way.

He gripped one of the shiny new door handles but didn't pull. He knew why he was hesitating. This was his tradition, his routine on the day of Natalie's death. Deep down, he knew this year was different. Up until now, there had been no other woman in his life since his late wife. Now that things had gotten serious with Hadley, he sensed there had been a cosmic shift in his perspective.

Taking a deep breath, he tugged the door on the exhale. It opened, and he stepped into the warmth of the vestibule, letting the door swing shut behind him. As he crossed over the soft burgundy carpet toward the sanctuary, he heard footsteps from the west hall.

Camille, the church secretary, approached with a smile on her face and a stack of papers in hand. The moment she saw him, she made a beeline for him and folded him in a hug. "Devon! How are you, son?"

He looked down at her, matching her smile. She was only about five feet tall, and well into her sixties. She had been church secretary from his earliest memories. "I'm good, Ms. Camille. How about you?"

She shrugged. "You know, I can't complain. The Lord is keeping me, my grandchildren are thriving and I still have my Sam. You know Celia lost Frank in the spring."

He nodded. "I heard about it. I sent flowers." Celia was Camille's twin sister and a gifted musician who served as the church's organist.

Camille stepped back then. "Well, I know why you're here, so I won't keep you. Stop in and see Reverend Keene before you leave, okay? He's been asking after you."

"I will, Ms. Camille." He leaned down to give her a peck on the cheek.

Still grinning, she left, passing him and disappearing down the east hall.

Turning back to the sanctuary doors, he pushed them open and entered. The space was as devoid of people as he'd expected. It was Wednesday, and all the happenings at the church that day were scheduled for the evening. He looked around, taking in the familiarity of the place. The lacquered oak pews with their red velvet–upholstered cushions still held a few scattered hymnals and programs from the Christmas Eve service. The scant sunlight filtered through the stained glass windows, casting a rainbow of colors on the hardwood floors.

Walking over the red carpet that spanned the center aisle, he quietly went to the first pew on the right, the one nearest to the altar. Sitting down, he looked up at the raised pulpit, his eyes finding the wall behind the choir stand. The painting there depicted a blue sky filled with puffy white clouds. The center-most cloud, the focal point of the image, held up two golden gates. A golden cross topped the gates, and a brilliant white light emanated from them.

He smiled, despite the melancholy that had brought him here. The painting was an artist's vision of heaven, and he liked to think Natalie was there, resting comfortably. Her last days had been trying, and his grief at losing her had been tempered with a sense of relief that she no longer suffered.

Alone on the pew, he let his memories of her wash over him. There were parts of his heart that would always hold her dear, but he knew his mother was right. The time had come to get off the "merry-go-round" and settle down again. Since he'd lost Natalie, being in a serious relationship had been the farthest thing from his mind. He'd taken a few women out for drinks, dancing or coffee. That had only led to zealous paparazzi snapping and publishing pictures to make him seem like a playboy. The reality was that no woman had really enamored him or captured his attention beyond the surface level since his late wife.

No woman until Hadley.

Now, in the silence, he grappled with this new reality. Hadley had worked her way into his heart, and he knew he couldn't stop it from happening. What really stood out about the situation was that he didn't *want* to stop himself from falling in love. Not this time. Hadley had effectively changed the way he looked at his life.

She'd touched his soul, reminding him that beneath his grief and his efforts to keep women at a distance, there was something else: loneliness. Somehow, she'd dug down into his very core and revealed his vulnerability. Yet for some reason, he trusted her not to take advantage of him.

Letting a sigh escape, he closed his eyes and dropped his head into his hands. He'd never thought this day would come, and now the stress of it had begun to get to him.

A voice echoed in the silence. "It's time, son."

Opening his eyes, he looked up toward the sound.

Reverend Keene stood to the left of the pulpit. Clad in the casual jeans and sweatshirt he often wore on weekdays, he rested his hand on the organ. The older man's deep brown face, punctuated by white whiskers, held concern and empathy. "I don't mean to interrupt, but I know why you're here."

Devon nodded. "It's not an interruption. Actually, I could use some counsel."

The minister walked over, taking a seat next to him on the pew. "You've done right by Nat, Devon. We all loved her, too. I know you've closed yourself off out of respect to her."

He shrugged. "I guess I have." Natalie had moved to Sapphire Shores with her family during Devon's seventh grade year, and remained until graduating high school, so she'd been well-known around the church, too.

Reverend Keene narrowed his eyes, observing Devon's face. "But this year, something's different. You met someone?"

Devon nodded. "I'm surprised you haven't heard about it, since the island's so small and close-knit."

"There's been some chatter around the fellowship hall, but you know I don't condone gossip." He winked. "Whatever the case, if you're closing your heart off to someone because of the specter of Natalie's memory, it's time to stop."

He looked at the man, who'd played a role in his upbringing, and felt the rightness of his words. "My mother said the same thing to me before I left LA."

"Eva's right. Remember what Ecclesiastes teaches us. 'To everything there is a season, and a time to every purpose under heaven.'" Reverend Keene patted Devon's shoulder as he stood again. "If the Lord has sent someone to touch your heart, then you know what it means. Okay, son?"

"Yes, sir." He watched as the minister walked down the aisle and through the sanctuary doors.

As he faced the pulpit again, his eyes settling on the image of heaven, Devon clasped his hands and let the guilt leave his body like a rising vapor. He tossed aside any concern for time, allowing himself to work through it all. He would never forget Natalie. Fortunately, moving on with his life didn't require him to do so.

Letting that settle into his spirit gave him the sense of peace he'd been seeking for the past five years. And when the lightness came over him, heralding his freedom from the negative feelings, he quietly left the church.

## Chapter 15

Hadley, dressed in an old pair of sweats and a T-shirt, curled up on her couch with her feet tucked beneath her. After busting her hump at work all last week, she'd finally started her winter vacation. With yesterday's holiday meal now out of the way, she was looking forward to spending her Wednesday night vegged out in front of the television. She had a glass of wine and big bowl of fresh popcorn next to her.

She grasped the remote, pointing it and flipping through the channels. Coming across a marathon of *Say Yes to the Dress*, she set the remote down and settled in. She loved this show. It amused her to watch women cry, scream and get all bent out of shape over a wedding dress. For the life of her, she couldn't fathom the level of emotion the women put into a piece of clothing, or how much money they were willing to drop on something they'd wear only once. When her day came, she planned to wear a simple white pantsuit and call it a day.

During the commercial break, she let her mind wander. She hadn't heard from Devon today, and she hadn't expected to. She could sense he'd been overwhelmed by her family during dinner. The barrage of questions from her dad and brothers, plus the all-out gusto with which the Monroes celebrated Christmas, had taken it out of him. While he'd been perfectly calm all afternoon, by the time he'd gone home for the night, he'd told her himself that he'd need a couple of days to himself to recuperate and recharge. She respected that. She'd never been one to cling to a man, and she didn't plan to start now.

Admittedly, she did miss him. She wondered what he was doing and how he was handling his meals all by himself. At any rate, she planned to leave him alone until he was ready.

The show was back on, and a bride was going on and on about how much she hated lace when Hadley heard a knock on the door of her apartment. Her brow furrowed, because she hadn't been expecting anyone to stop by. Clambering up from her comfortable position, she padded to the door and checked the peephole.

Savion stood on the concrete balcony, tapping his foot impatiently.

Opening the door, she asked, "What are you doing here? You couldn't call first?"

He leaned against the door frame, looking over her

head into the apartment. "Why? You're not doing anything except bingeing on TV and snacks."

"Whatever." Rolling her eyes, she stepped aside to let him in.

He flopped down on the couch, gesturing to her popcorn. "May I?"

"Yeah, go ahead." She joined him, tucking her body against the right armrest while he sat on the left-most cushion, munching on her snack.

"Is this that wedding dress–shopping show?" he asked around a mouthful of popcorn.

She folded her arms over her chest. "Savion."

He shrugged. "What?"

She gave him a playful punch on the arm. "I know you didn't come here to watch TV with me, so what do you want?"

"I want to know what's going on between you and Devon." He looked pointedly at her as he chewed, waiting for her answer.

"I don't see how that's any of your business." She was already annoyed by his showing up without calling, eating her snack and interrupting her show.

"You're my baby sister, and it's my business now and any other time I think you might be in danger—"

"Danger? From Devon?" That seemed a bit farfetched. They hadn't been at this dating thing long, but he'd always treated her well. Devon was, as the classic Ralph Tresvant song proclaimed, a stone-cold gentleman.

He rolled his eyes and set the popcorn bowl aside. "I

don't mean physical danger—unless you come across one of his overzealous groupies."

She side-eyed him. "Really, Savion?"

"Don't you know what you're dealing with here?" Savion shook his head, his expression reading as if he knew something she didn't. "Devon is a big action star. He probably gets panties thrown at him everywhere he goes."

"That's really crude." She tried to push away the imagery of her brother's rather blunt statement. She had no desire to contemplate the number or the types of propositions Devon received from random women on the street. She would then question whether she could compete with those women, which in turn led down the rabbit hole of doubt.

"Still, you have to admit women are probably sweating him all the time." He sat back against the sofa cushions. "Plus, if you read the blogs, you'd know he has a bit of a, shall we say, reputation. Campbell knows about it, too."

"Oh, please." She was shocked her serious, staid brother would even admit to reading trashy online gossip. "If you and Cam spent more time working and less time on the internet, my life would be a whole hell of a lot easier."

Savion's face folded into a frown. "Baby sis, I'm sure you're not implying that Cam and I are lazy." He fixed her with a searching look.

She pursed her lips. "You're right, I'm not trying to imply that. I'm saying it straight-out. Y'all are lazy."

He cut his eyes at her, as if she would rescind her statement if he eyeballed her hard enough.

Undeterred, she stared at him. "Lazy. L-a-z-y. You're not lacking in skill, you just leave entirely too much of the work around the office to me."

He sighed. "Cam does, I'll admit that."

"How charitable." She was quickly growing tired of her brother's foolishness.

"I give you more because I'm so busy. Every time I turn around, there's some executive decision to be made, a call to take or something to sign off on. You're more than capable, though."

"Savion, don't patronize me or else—"

"I'm sorry, Hadley. I'm not trying to insult you." He gave her a crooked smile. "I never thought much about it until now, but you do a lot."

"You're damn straight. And despite everything I do, you and Cam still treat me like a little girl. You ignore my suggestions, talk over me and in general make my workday difficult." She watched his face, seeing the guilt playing over it, and felt a modicum of vindication.

"But I didn't—"

She wasn't hearing any of it. "And now you have the gall to come here, to my home, and tell me what to do in my personal life."

His eyes widened. "Hadley, I didn't realize—"

She pinched her fingers together in midair. "Clam up, Savion. I'm tired, and all I want to do is watch TV in peace. You're welcome to think about everything I've said…on your way out." She pointed at the door, beyond ready for her brother's departure.

He stood, strode to the door. Opening it, he started to go out, then stopped and turned back. "Hadley, I know Cam and I can drive you crazy—Dad, too, probably. But remember, it's just because we love you so much."

"I love you, too." She winked, then shooed him out. "Now go love me from a distance."

Chuckling, he stepped outside and shut the door behind him.

Shaking her head, Hadley grabbed her popcorn and went back to watching her show.

*These Monroe men are such a handful.*

When Devon got up, he quickly got himself together then headed to the kitchen for some cereal. With his bowl and mug of coffee, he sat down to enjoy his breakfast and the morning silence.

While he ate, he used his tablet to check emails. He perked up when he saw that all the contacts he'd emailed about helping him find a lead for a directing gig had replied. The feeling was short-lived, though, because none of the three respondents could help—or were willing to. Two of them went into the reasons why they didn't have anything for him, citing his reputation as an action star and nothing more. The third hadn't even bothered to write out a sentence, and instead had responded with a single phrase: LOL. Closing his email program, Devon slid the tablet away and returned his attention to his breakfast.

He thought back on the conversation he'd had with Glenn about branching out on his own. Glenn had been right—if Devon owned his own production company, no one could stop him from directing. So far, every contact he'd reached out to had either refused him help or made jokes about his dreams. At this point, he only hoped no one had mounted a campaign to actively block him from being part of the industry.

*What would I need to open a production company? Where would I even start?* He knew he'd need a building with space for offices, soundstages and more. He'd have to decide where this company would be headquartered. Then there would be staff to hire, projects to vet and more. Draining the last of his coffee, he decided to put a pin in it. This was a big undertaking, and it was just too damn early in the morning to be thinking this hard about anything.

As he set his empty bowl in the sink, a knock at the front door broke the silence. He went to answer it and was surprised to find Campbell standing on his doorstep. He opened the door, letting in a blast of cold air. "Hey, Cam. What's up?"

"What's up, Dev. Can I come in for a minute?" He stood with a stooped, closed posture, as if hiding from the wind. "It's cold as hell out here."

He stepped back. "Yeah, come on. I'm not gonna just stand here letting all that icy wind in the house." Once Campbell was inside, Devon shut the door and gestured to the couch. "Have a seat, man."

"Thanks." Cam shrugged off his black parka and sat down.

"What brings you over?" He couldn't help but wonder why Campbell was there so early on a weekday.

He knew MHI's office was closed until the second of January, but he hadn't expected Campbell to stop by.

"I just wanted to talk to you really quick. Shouldn't take too long."

Curiosity furrowed his brow. "Is it about the property?"

Campbell shook his head. "Nah."

"Okay." Realizing he should be hospitable, Devon added, "You want something to drink? Coffee, maybe?"

He shook his head again.

By now Devon was plenty interested in knowing what had brought his friend to the town house. "So, say what you gotta say, man."

Scratching his chin, Campbell looked at him. "It's about you and Hadley."

*Ah, hell.* Brow furrowed, Devon waited. He should have expected this. After he'd spent most of Christmas dinner with the other two Monroe men interrogating him, now it seemed Cam wanted a shot.

"I'm not trying to tell you what to do. You're grown." He paused, took a breath. "But things between Hadley and Pops are not great. And I know she's also not too pleased with Savion."

He folded his arms over his chest. "But you're on good terms with her, I assume?"

Campbell nodded. "I had sense enough not to say anything to her. Plus, I already told you, I don't have a problem with you two seeing each other."

"I see."

"Anyway, I'm sure you remember how they acted on

Christmas. And then Savion took it upon himself to go over to her house yesterday and lecture her."

A snorting laugh escaped Devon's lips. "Why in the hell would he do that?"

With a shrug, Cam surmised, "Because he's a glutton for punishment? I don't know. Everybody who knows my sister knows she's her own woman."

Devon chuckled as he imagined what had gone down at Hadley's place when Savion had shown up, trying to tell her what to do. "How hard did she hit him?"

This time Campbell laughed. "Lucky for him, she didn't. But she did kick him out."

While this whole thing was amusing, he still didn't see the connection. "Okay, I hear what you're saying. But what does that have to do with you being here?"

"With all that's going on, I have to ask you. How serious are you about my sister?"

"Very." Devon could see his entire future in Hadley's eyes. "More serious than I've ever been about anyone."

Campbell sighed. "I guess that means you're not going to back off, then."

He shook his head. "Nope. But why would you ask me to? You've told me more than once that you don't have a problem with us dating."

"Personally, I don't. Still, I hate to see all this drama going on between my family members." Campbell ran his hand through his beard. "You know me. I'm not one for drama."

Devon nodded. Even back in high school, Campbell had avoided conflict whenever he could and had been known for stepping in to break up arguments and scuffles.

"I'm not backing down. I love your sister, and I've already told her as much. I'm in this thing, all the way."

Campbell's expression was one of resignation. "Just thought I'd ask. If you love her, she'll be worth the fight, right?"

"She already is." He locked eyes with his friend so he could convey his seriousness. "She's everything I want, everything I need."

"Wow. Never heard anyone speak about Hadley that way before." He clapped his hands together and stood. "I'm not going to take sides if the crap hits the fan, you know."

"I know." He didn't expect Cam to do something that went against the core of who he was.

"I'm still cool with this relationship. Not that y'all need my permission." He stretched, then reached for his parka. "I suggest you gird your loins to do battle with Savion and Pops. But you'll have no trouble out of me."

Standing, Devon extended his closed fist toward Campbell. "Thanks, man."

Bumping fists with him, Campbell headed for the door. "No problem. I'll let myself out."

Devon waved as Campbell opened the door and walked out, shutting it behind him.

# Chapter 16

Friday morning, Hadley sat in her usual seat at the conference room table, tapping a pen on the lacquered surface. She knew her face was scrunched into a frown, but she didn't care. It was a few days after Christmas, and she should still be home enjoying her vacation. Instead, because the reps from Neville South couldn't wait to make their pitch, she and her brothers were at the office.

Savion, seated at the head of the table on Hadley's right, was busy flipping through the full-color proposal the developer had sent over. He'd been engrossed in the booklet for the last fifteen minutes.

She cut her eyes extra hard in Savion's direction. He was the one who'd caved to the developer's offer to hold the meeting today, taking away a full day of her vacation.

Campbell sat across from her, scrolling through something on his phone. He hadn't been particularly happy about coming in today, either. Now he seemed to be making a show of his disinterest by refusing to look up from his phone.

Hadley, on the other hand, intended to redeem the time, as her grandmother used to say. If she had to sacrifice her hard-earned vacation time, she wasn't going to waste the opportunity to be heard. She looked at the folder she'd brought with her, lying on the table next to where she'd been tapping her pen. Her brothers had no idea of the contents of the folder, and she planned to keep it that way until the right moment.

Campbell's phone buzzed, loud in the quiet of the room. After a few taps on his screen, he said, "The people from Neville South are here."

Savion smiled and stood. "I'll go let them in." He disappeared from the room.

Arms folded over her chest, Hadley waited for the developer's salespeople to appear. She expected they'd come in grinning, all ready to win her over with their carefully crafted pitch.

*Nope. I'm not having any of it.* She'd already heard everything she needed to know she was against the proposal. Since Savion had set up the meeting, she supposed the polite thing to do would be to let them talk for a while before she made her play.

Savion entered the room again then, followed by two men in dark suits. One was fair-haired, with blue eyes. The other had skin the color of milk chocolate and brown eyes that seemed to be assessing everyone in the room—Hadley noticed the way his gaze lingered on her.

Hadley and Campbell each stood. Gesturing to the two newcomers, Savion introduced them. "This is Alvin Clark—" he motioned to the Black man "—and this is Gordon Young."

Handshakes were exchanged, and Hadley almost had to pry her hand from Alvin's grasp. She kept her expression even, but her eyes let him know, plainly, that she wasn't playing games.

Once everyone was seated at the table, with Gordon sitting next to Hadley and Alvin next to Campbell, the presentation began in earnest. Gordon laid out maps and concept drawings on the table, droning on about landscaping and parking.

Campbell seemed to be paying attention, offering a nod or a short comment here and there. Savion appeared enraptured by all the concept drawings, even though he'd already seen them. Hadley closed her eyes momentarily, thinking of all the effort that had gone into the materials, yet unable to muster much interest.

Then Alvin took over, presenting his charts and graphs of expected revenue from the new development. "As you can see, both Neville South and Monroe Holdings stand to turn a tidy profit. We think this development will be immensely beneficial for both our companies."

Savion's eyes lit up at the phrase *tidy profit*.

Hadley sighed. Her brother wasn't a greedy person, but he was fastidious in his efforts to increase revenue and decrease expenses for Monroe Holdings. This part of the presentation seemed to tap into his greatest desire: to make MHI as profitable as it had been under their father's leadership.

As if to put a finer point on the potential financial gain, Alvin continued, "We think this development will be immensely beneficial for both our companies. The location is perfect for a venture like this, and with Gordon and his team handling the aesthetics, people will be drawn to it in droves."

Their concerns seem to rest solely on profit, and therein lay the problem. Hadley felt the frown creeping over her face. The time had come for her to make a stand before her brother signed over the land. "Excuse me, Mr. Clark—"

He stopped her with his raised hand. "Please, call me Alvin."

"Fine, Alvin. I've heard a lot about how much money our two companies can make from this development. What I haven't heard is how it will help the island's citizens. Can you elaborate on that?" She sat back in her chair, awaiting his answer.

Savion shot her a dirty look.

Hadley didn't care.

Alvin cleared his throat. "Well, Ms. Monroe, that's a great question. Of course, the development will bring jobs to the island. People will be needed in the shops and restaurants, as well as to maintain the condominiums. We estimate two hundred positions will be created by the—"

"Yes, I heard that before. Two hundred jobs, most of them paying at or below minimum wage. What do you have to say about what seems like a concerted effort to keep local businesses from becoming tenants in the shopping center?"

Blinking rapidly, Alvin stammered. "I…well, we plan to allow new businesses to come and—"

"And what about existing businesses? We have plenty of skilled entrepreneurs already here, and I think shutting them out of the development is misguided and downright wrong." She rested her elbows on the table and tented her fingers. "What do you have to say about that?"

Alvin's eyes registered panic. He looked to Gordon, who only shrugged.

Savion raised his hand. "Okay, Hadley. I realize you're passionate about this, but let's not attack our guests."

She glanced at her brothers, then at the developer's mouthpieces. "I'm not attacking anyone. I'm simply asking pertinent questions. I don't know why these two gentlemen would come here unprepared to answer them."

Alvin remarked, "I wouldn't say we're unprepared."

She smiled the smirk of a woman about to make a point. "Fine. Let's just say you're uninformed." She opened the folder and took out the copies of her petition. "This is a petition signed by almost three hundred of the island's citizens. All of them are opposed to the construction of Neville South's development. A few have even lodged complaints with the town council." She riffled through her papers. "I have copies of the complaints as well, if you'd like to see them."

The four sets of male eyes around the table widened.

Hadley sat back, waiting.

Campbell chuckled. "That's our girl. Kicking ass and taking names."

Savion frowned. "Why didn't you tell me about this, Hadley? And when did you even have time to start a petition?"

"I tried to tell you. You just weren't interested in hearing anything that didn't line up with your vision." She turned back to Alvin and Gordon. "Would you like to see the town council complaints, gentlemen?"

Gordon shook his head. "That won't be necessary."

Alvin, already on his feet, gathered up his charts. "Considering what we've just learned, I think we'd better postpone any major moves on this project, Mr. Monroe."

Savion nodded. "I agree. We'll reconvene after the New Year."

Gordon took a moment to roll up his images, and after that, he and his partner left in a hurry.

After they were gone, Savion turned to her. "Hadley, you are something else. You're determined to stop this development, aren't you?"

She winked. "I thought I'd made that clear, Savion." Satisfied that her point was made, she gathered her copies back into the folder. "Now I'd like to continue my vacation, if you don't mind."

"Go ahead." Savion waved her out.

The still-amused Campbell remarked, "You're a real pistol, sis."

Smiling as she carried her purse and folder to the conference room door, she tossed back, "Damn straight." Then she strode out.

Devon had just parked in the MHI lot when he saw Hadley marching out of the double glass doors. Gathering the dozen blush-pink roses he'd brought with him from the passenger seat, he climbed out of the car, careful not to damage the blooms.

He took a moment to enjoy the view of the beautiful woman he called his own. She had the sexiest walk of any woman he'd ever seen. He could almost hear "Love's Theme," the classic instrumental by Barry White's Love Unlimited Orchestra, playing in his head as he watched her. She was dressed in a white blouse and a pair of fitted gray trousers that hugged her bottom nicely. Her black pumps clicked on the pavement in time with her steps. Her soft curls were tucked up into a high bun, giving him a full view of the graceful lines of her face—which was scrunched into a perturbed frown. He couldn't help but be concerned.

*What's going on with her?* He adjusted the flowers, the plastic overwrap crinkling as he tucked them into the crook of his arm. He quickened his steps, aiming to meet her on the sidewalk.

She looked his way then, and her expression softened considerably and surprise lit her eyes. Slowing her steps, she stopped and waited for him until he stepped up on the curb. Leaning up, she gave him a peck on the lips. "Devon, what are you doing here?"

He handed her the flowers, which were miraculously still standing up despite the unusually high humidity. "When you texted me that you had to come in on vacation, you seemed upset. So I thought I'd try to lift your mood."

"You're so sweet." She smiled, but only for a moment before the frown returned.

He asked, "What, you don't like pink?"

She shook her head. "It's not that. The roses are beautiful. It's just that you just reminded me that I forgot my phone."

"Inside the office?"

She nodded.

"That's an easy fix. Just go back in and grab it."

She pursed her lips. "I've had enough of Savion for the day. Let me borrow your phone. I'll call Cam and ask him to bring it out."

He shrugged, dragging his phone from his pocket and passing it to her. "Sure thing."

While he waited, she called her brother and asked him to bring out her phone. Then she passed the phone back to him. "Thanks."

He tucked the phone away again. "So, how did the meeting go?"

She smiled then, making his heart sing. "I think it went pretty great. Remember the petition against the development I spent last Saturday gathering signatures for?"

"You spent most of the day on it."

"Yep. I knew most of the places downtown would

have a good amount of business on a Saturday afternoon."

"Very astute. I see why you were so insistent on leaving."

She nodded. "It was my last chance at gathering that many signatures before we went on holiday vacation. I didn't expect to have to put the petition to use until after the New Year, but Neville South insisted on this early meeting."

"I see." He remembered how she'd left that morning, after they'd made love all night and well into the wee hours. The memories of her lush nudity rose again then, and he licked his lower lip. *She's a hell of a woman.*

Her lips kept moving, indicating she was saying something.

Most of what she'd said went underwater, as he struggled to focus. Visions of her beneath him, moaning as he stroked her, were making it difficult for him to keep his attention on the present. "I'm sorry, baby. What did you say?"

She laughed and gave him a playful punch on the shoulder. "Stop daydreaming and listen this time."

He placed his hand over his heart. "I promise I will."

"Anyway, I had said that I hadn't told anybody in the office...until today, when I slapped it down on the table during the presentation. You should have seen the looks on those guys' faces." She seemed pleased with herself. "Then they packed up their stuff and got out of here quick. It was pretty epic."

Chuckling, he gave her shoulder a squeeze. "I'm

proud of you. You saw a problem and tried to fix it. And when the first try didn't work, you didn't give up."

Her smile grew broader. "Thanks, Devon. You know, I owe this to you. You pushed me to keep at it, even when it looked pretty grim."

He looked at her, amazed at her determination. "I never would have thought of the petition, but I'm glad you did it. What a way to get your point across."

"So I have you to blame for this?" A male voice cut into their conversation.

Both Devon and Hadley swiveled toward the voice.

Savion stood on the sidewalk a couple of feet away, brow furrowed. He stuck out his hand toward his sister. "Here's your phone."

Rolling her eyes, she took the device and dropped it into her purse. "I thought Cam was bringing it."

"I was on my way out," Savion said before swinging his eyes back to Devon. "So you're the one who's been encouraging her in this crusade against progress?"

Devon turned toward him. "Not really. She was just following her convictions, and I'm behind her one hundred percent."

"You'd deny the islanders this shot at hundreds of new jobs, more housing and more tourism revenue? Just to get brownie points with my sister?" He folded his arms over his chest.

"This isn't about brownie points."

"Oh, yeah? Then why do you care either way?" Savion walked a few steps closer. "You haven't lived here full-time in over a decade. Why are you suddenly so concerned about what happens to the island?"

Devon rubbed his hands together. "That was a low blow, Savion."

Savion shrugged. "Truth hurts."

Hadley snapped, "Savion, enough of this."

Shaking his head, Devon touched her shoulder. "Don't worry, baby. I've got this." He turned back toward Savion. "Look, I grew up here, too. Where I live now has nothing to do with the fact that I care about Sapphire Shores and the people who do live here year-round."

"Yeah, right." Savion tapped his foot, as if growing impatient. "I've been over the numbers and statistics more than once, and I'm telling you, this development is just what the island needs."

Rolling his eyes, Devon remarked, "There are two sides to every argument. Just because you feel a certain way, that doesn't mean it's right."

"I could say the same thing to you." Savion gave him a hard stare.

They stood there in silence for a few long moments, observing each other. Hadley looked somewhat uncomfortable, but she didn't interfere.

Devon sensed Savion was waiting for him to back down, but it wasn't going to happen. Placing his hand on the small of Hadley's back, he stood his ground. "We can agree to disagree on this. But if you expect me to change sides or run away because you're eyeballing me, you're sadly mistaken."

"That's how it is, Devon?"

He cocked his head to one side. "That's exactly how it is." With that, he turned away from Savion, done with the conversation. He stooped to kiss Hadley on the cheek. "I'll see you later, baby." Then he turned and strode back to his car.

He could feel Savion's eyes on his back, but he didn't turn around.

# Chapter 17

That night, Hadley knocked on the door of Devon's town house. When he opened the door and stepped out onto the porch, she greeted him with a smile. "You look handsome, Devon." She made no effort to hide the fact that she was ogling him. Dressed in brown slacks, a tan button-down shirt and tan-and-brown loafers, he had a brown sport coat tossed over his shoulder.

He leaned down, placing a soft kiss on her lips. "You look gorgeous, as always." Holding her hand, he stepped down off the porch. "Here, do a little turn for me, baby."

Blushing, she executed a full 360-degree turn, showing off the long-sleeved shimmering gold sweater dress she wore. "I'm glad you like it."

As they walked toward her car, he remarked, "You

know, you didn't have to do this. I don't expect you to apologize for Savion."

She nodded, tapping the button on her keys to unlock the car doors. "I know. But I still feel bad about the way he sniped at you today."

He shrugged. "I get it. That's how a classy woman rolls. And I'll gladly accompany your fine ass to dinner, whatever the reason." He winked, going to the driver's side and opening the door for her.

She climbed in and buckled up while he closed the door and went around to his side. Once they were both in the car and strapped in, she backed out of the driveway and headed down the road.

Hadley kept her eyes ahead as the car moved through the darkened streets. Devon's large hand rested on her thigh as she drove, sending tingles of anticipation dancing over her skin. Soft R & B music poured from the stereo system, the lyrics reminding her of what she'd like most for dessert. Oceanview Grill boasted an extensive selection of desserts, but only Devon's loving could satisfy her sweet tooth. A smile tilted her lips as she thought of all the ways she wanted to savor him.

Once they reached the restaurant, she parked and he escorted her inside. The heavenly aromas of the woodburning grill and the fresh herbs used to season the food greeted her the moment they entered. She'd anticipated the Friday night crowd, and had made a reservation to ensure they'd get a table without a long wait. The place was just as packed as she'd expected it to be, and the din of various conversations and silverware clanging against dishes echoed through the interior.

The hostess escorted them to a booth along the back wall, where the windows looked out on the sand dunes and the beach.

Seated in the booth, Hadley picked up her menu. "Maybe I'll try something new this time. Have you ever had red snapper?"

"Yeah. There's a place in LA that makes a fantastic broiled red snapper." His gaze rested on his own menu as he spoke. "I'm in the mood for something else, though. Maybe surf and turf."

When the waiter came by with their glasses of water and the basket of rolls, she looked up from the menu. "We're still deciding. Can you swing back in a few minutes?"

"Of course." The waiter left to take care of his other tables.

"I think I'm gonna just do the surf and turf." Devon sat his menu aside. "Listen, can I talk to you about something?"

Reading the seriousness on his face, she put her own menu down. "Sure, what is it?"

He drew a breath. "I spent some time over at Mt. Ephraim on Wednesday."

She nodded. "I know. You go there every year on December 26."

One of his thick brows hitched up. "How do you know that?"

She shrugged. "Small island. Plus, my parents still go to that church."

"If you know about my trips, then you probably know why I go. Natalie passed on December 26, and going there every year has been my way of dealing with my grief. I'm not all that religious, but it really has helped to go there, pray and reflect."

"I understand." She felt honored that he would share something so personal with her.

"This year was a little different," he continued. "It's the first time I've gone when I've been seriously involved with someone, and—"

She reached across the table, grabbed his hands. "I don't mean to cut you off, but I love you, Devon, and it's high time I told you."

A broad smile spread over his face. "I'm glad to hear that, because..."

Hadley's eyes drifted from Devon's face as a familiar yet disturbing feeling came over her. The feeling of being watched. Sure enough, when she looked around, she saw a man sitting across from them, alone in a booth. The man was attempting to be discreet, but it was obvious he was watching them over his menu. "Devon, I think you've got a fan in here."

He chuckled. "Maybe so. We'll wait and see if they come over and ask for an autograph."

She swung her gaze back to her handsome companion, pushing away the creepy feeling she got from the menu watcher.

"What were you saying, Devon?"

"I was saying that I had a talk with Reverend Keene, and I think it's time I moved on and—"

Shouting broke out at the hostess stand, and both Hadley and Devon turned in that direction.

A tall dark-haired man, wearing a camera on a strap

around his neck, was arguing with the hostess. As the man's hands flailed around, he seemed to be gesturing toward Devon's table.

Devon frowned. "That guy looks familiar."

"Someone you've worked with?"

Shaking his head, Devon's frown deepened. "He's a paparazzo. But what the hell is he doing here?"

Tension crept into Hadley's shoulders. Something told her that things were about to go sideways, in a big way.

A flash went off to her right, by the window.

Swiveling her head, Hadley's eyes grew wide when she saw two photographers crouched outside the restaurant window. "Shit."

Devon was already on his feet. "You can say that again. Let's get the hell out of here."

Grabbing her purse, she took his hand and the two of them darted across the restaurant. Hadley's heel caught on a tablecloth, dragging the dishes set up on the unoccupied table to the floor. She heard the crash and cringed but didn't stop.

They flew past the hostess stand, with both the menu watcher and the hostess harasser on their tail. More flashes went off around them, illuminating the blurred scenery as they ducked into Hadley's car.

The menu watcher shouted, "Miss Monroe! Why would you tip us off it you didn't want to be photographed?"

"I don't know what you're talking about!" She called back just as loudly.

While they buckled up, some of the photographers

circled close to the car. More shouted questions were thrown at them.

"Is it true you two are an item?"

"Devon, will you be returning to LA?"

Hadley turned the engine over and looked directly ahead. Her eyes communicated that she was leaving, but just in case, she tapped the gas pedal to rev the engine.

The photographers backed away, and Hadley peeled out of the lot.

For the first few minutes of their escape from the photographers, Devon looked out the window, watching the scenery roll by. He'd thrown on his sport jacket while they'd been rushing out of Oceanview Grill, to stave off the wintry chill in the air. Now, trapped in the car with the heat flowing from the vents and the tension snapping between the two of them, he wished he could take it off again. In his mind, he wondered how he'd ended up in a situation like this. He'd been coming back home for years now and had never been harassed by photographers before. The whole reason he chose his hometown for his vacation was peace and quiet, but that concept had certainly been shattered tonight.

He waited, thinking that if he gave Hadley time, she'd apologize for calling in those media goons. As he tried to settle his racing pulse, he retreated into his own thoughts. He had so many unanswered questions about what had just happened, and all of them centered on Hadley. His familiarity with the photos-for-profit crowd was surface level, but he knew enough. Candid shots were worth far more than posed ones. The photographers knew that and would do anything to get their next high-paying shot. Paying someone who had intel on where celebrities would be wasn't outside their comfort zone.

So, was that why had Hadley summoned them here? *How much are they paying her?*

*What did she have to gain by alerting them to my whereabouts?*

Several blocks away from the restaurant, Devon looked at Hadley. "What just happened?"

"I don't know." She seemed bit out of breath. "I never expected anything like this."

His face creased into a frown. Was her expectation a subtle admission of her guilt in all this? "Even though you called them?"

Stopped at a red light, she turned to stare at him. "Devon, I didn't call anyone."

"One of the reporters said you tipped them off." How would the guy even know her name if she wasn't the one who'd dimed him out?

The light changed, and she went through the intersection. "He's lying. I never contacted anyone. Why would I do that?"

"I don't know, Hadley."

"Besides, I'm not the only one who knows you're in town."

"Yeah, okay." He didn't bother to hide the impatience in his tone.

Her brow furrowed. "Come on, Devon. Plenty of people have seen you this year, and most folks on the island know you come every year around this time."

If he weren't so irritated, he would have laughed. "That's true. But the fact remains that in all the years I've been coming here, no one has bothered me up until now."

"That's true, but—"

He cut her off. "And today, when this crap happened, the only name mentioned was yours." His face was now tight with anger. It seemed she was determined to deny her involvement in this whole mess, but he was going to see to it that she took responsibility for her actions.

Her expression was a mixture of sadness and confusion. "Devon, I don't know what's going on, but I swear I didn't—"

He held up his hand. It had become clear that she wasn't going to admit to anything, and that meant there was no point in continuing this fruitless conversation. "Don't say anything else, please. Just drop me off at the town house."

Her jaw tightened, but she did as he asked, lapsing into silence.

He kept his eyes on the horizon, not even wanting to look at her. After everything they'd shared, how could she do this to him? He'd opened his heart to her in a way he hadn't with any woman since Natalie. And now she betrayed him this way? Calling in the same overzealous photographers who chased him around Los Angeles so they could infringe on his privacy there? He depended on his three-week vacation on the island to restore his peace of mind after the other forty-nine weeks spent on the left coast depleted it. Now, not only had he lost the woman he'd come to love, but he'd lost the one place he'd considered sacred. And it had all gone down in one night. He sighed, mourning everything that had been taken from him.

When she pulled up to the curb in front of the town house, he climbed out. "I'm leaving on the next available flight. My assistant will make sure the bill is handled."

Tears began to fill her eyes. "Devon, please."

He said nothing more. Though her tears moved him, activating the part of his heart that belonged to her and longed to comfort her, he quashed the urge. She couldn't be trusted, and he wouldn't be in a relationship with someone he couldn't trust.

He turned his back to her and started walking. Every step increased the physical distance between them, and he felt the emotional distance growing along with it.

He heard her crying behind him. But he didn't turn around. He wouldn't.

By the time he reached the front porch of the town house and inserted the key in the lock, he heard her switch the car into gear.

Only when he heard her drive away did he look back at the spot where she'd been parked.

Clenching his fist, he pushed open the door and went inside, shutting the door behind him. Shrugging out of his sport coat, he tossed it over the back of the couch and cracked his knuckles. The first order of business was to adjust his travel arrangements. He'd planned to stay on the island until after the New Year, but not anymore.

Settled in on the couch, he took out his phone and dialed Mimi, his assistant. Young, driven and something of a workaholic, she rarely took vacations and always answered his calls. He tried not to take advantage of her ambition, but this particular request couldn't wait.

He held the phone against his ear, waiting through two rings before she answered.

"Hello? What do you need, Mr. Granger?"

"Hi, Mimi. Can you please change my flight for me?"

She chuckled. "Sure thing. You wanna stay longer and enjoy some more relaxation?" The keys on her computer clicked as she began typing.

He frowned. "Afraid not. I need you to book me on the next available flight. And make sure my bill for the rental property is settled."

She paused, and when she spoke again, she sounded surprised. "Okay, I'll handle it. But as far as the flight goes, on this short notice, tickets will be hard to come by if you go commercial."

"That's fine. You know I don't do private jets." He considered the small aircraft, outfitted with wet bars and televisions, to be a wasteful extravagance. He made enough money to own a jet, but practicality ruled his spending, and he just couldn't muster the desire for one.

"You may even have to fly coach," she continued. "Is that okay?"

"That's fine." He wasn't the kind of guy who thought himself too good to fly coach. He'd be just fine alongside the regular Joes and Janes, traveling for work and play. "Do what you have to do to get me on a flight. Email me the details when you're done." He ended the call and went to pack his things.

The faster he got out of Sapphire Shores, the better.

## Chapter 18

The last Saturday night of the year found Hadley on her couch in a camisole and fuzzy pajama pants. All over the island, folks were celebrating, if the fireworks she heard in the distance were any indication. Usually she'd be out with Belinda and her girls. They'd all be enjoying a glass of wine on the beach, reveling in one another's company.

Her blowup with Devon last night had left her feeling anything but celebratory. She'd spent most of the morning calling and texting him, hoping he'd answer. She had to get him to listen, to hear her out. Apparently, he didn't want to talk, because her efforts had been ignored.

Now, curled up with the remote and her misery, she brushed away the tears yet again. She'd managed to screw things up with Devon, and she didn't even know how she'd done it.

Her front door swung open then, startling her. She yelped in surprise, but relaxed when she saw Belinda walk in. Her best friend had a key to her apartment, which explained her ability to get in, but not her sudden appearance.

Hadley sat up, using the tail of her top to dry her cheeks. "What are you doing here, B?"

"Girl, please. You think I couldn't tell something was wrong when I called you this morning?" She moved farther into the apartment, shifting the grocery bags she was carrying. "The better question is, what's wrong with you?"

She sighed. "Plenty. Close the door and I'll tell you all about it."

Belinda shook her head. "I can't close it yet. Somebody else is coming up."

Hadley's eyes shifted to the door as her ears picked up the sound of another pair of feet climbing the stairs outside. "Who else is coming? I'm in no mood for a party."

Belinda rolled her eyes. "Hush, Hadley. I wasn't sure how big the problem was, so like any good friend, I called in reinforcements."

And as Belinda finished her statement, Viola entered through the open door. Her eyes went straight to Hadley's. "Oh, Lord. What's wrong? Who's made my baby cry?"

For once, Hadley appreciated her mother's tendency toward babying her; she could certainly use the comfort right now. Standing, she went to her mother and let herself be enfolded in her soothing hug. She managed to hold back her tears until Belinda dropped her bags and joined them. That set her off again, and the tears flowed anew.

They separated and went to sit down. Hadley sat between her mother and her best friend, who occupied opposite ends of the couch. Once she was composed enough to speak, she took a deep breath. "Let's just say things have crashed and burned between me and Devon."

Belinda's lips curved downward. "Oh, no."

"Oh, yes." Hadley sniffled. "It happened last night, and he's been ignoring my calls and texts all day."

Viola, who sat shaking her head, asked, "What could have happened? Y'all looked so sweet together when he was over to the house for Christmas dinner."

She remembered well; it had only been a few days ago. *How did things go so wrong between us in such a short span of time?* "I don't really know myself. But he's probably back on the West Coast by now, because when he got out of the car, he told me he was leaving right away."

Belinda groaned. "That's why my housekeeping crew got a call today. He must have checked out of the town house."

Hadley had known he was leaving, but for some reason, hearing Belinda confirm it only made her sadder. "Damn."

Viola tilted her head to the side. "Hadley, just tell us what happened and we'll try to help you figure things out."

Inhaling deeply, Hadley gave them a rundown of her date with Devon, including the sneak attack mounted by the photographers. "One of them claimed the tip about Devon's location came from me. That's outrageous, because I never contacted anyone."

Belinda looked genuinely confused. "So how did these people get your name?"

She shrugged. "I don't have a clue. I've been asking myself that ever since I dropped Devon off. But I swear, I didn't contact them. I know he comes here for peace and quiet. I would never do that to him, even if we weren't dating." Saying that aloud reminded her that they were no longer a couple; he'd made that clear with his cold manner last night, and solidified it by ignoring her attempts to reach him.

Touching her shoulder, Belinda gave her a sad smile. "I'm sorry, Hadley. This is a tough one."

"You're telling me." She sank back against the overstuffed cushions, trying to fight off the rising sadness. "After all this time pining after Devon, I finally get the courage to tell him how I feel. And after a week and a half of absolute bliss, this happens. Just when it seems we're making a real connection."

Viola patted her thigh. "At least your conscience is clean. If you say you didn't contact those people, I believe you. I raised you better than to lie."

Hadley blew out a breath, struggling against the emotions roiling around inside her. "In the short time we were together, he did so much for me. I mean, I never would have thought to petition against the Neville South development if he hadn't encouraged me not to give up."

"Wow." The usually stoic Belinda seemed impressed.

"Yeah. He pushed me to stand up for my convictions,

even when it became hard to do so. Aside from that, he was such a gentleman. He treated me like a queen. Opened doors, pulled out chairs, the whole deal." She shook her head ruefully. "What am I going to do now that he's gone?"

Viola stood then. "I'll tell you what I'm going to do. I'm going to stop sitting on the sidelines about this Neville South development."

Hadley looked up at her mother. "Mom, I love you so much. But if you're going to side with Daddy and Savion, you're welcomed to keep sitting this one out." She couldn't take any more bad news right now.

Viola pursed her lips. "Oh, hush, child. I'm on your side. Truth is, this development is too big for a place as small as Sapphire Shores. I've lived here for forty years, and I can see this deal for what it is. The benefits aren't worth the traffic headaches, litter and increase in property taxes it will also bring."

That triggered a small smile for Hadley. "So, if the Monroe men stand their ground on this…"

Viola clapped her hands together. "Then you and I go into battle together, honey. Your father needs to be contradicted now and then, and he's about due."

Refreshed by her mother's declaration, Hadley nodded. "I appreciate that, Mom. I really do." This was the first time she could remember her mother standing firm on something that was in direct opposition to her father. Knowing Carver Monroe, and how stubborn he could be, Hadley assumed it wasn't easy for her mother to do this. "But what am I going to do about Devon?"

Belinda piped up. "Now, this is my wheelhouse. As

your best friend, I'm gonna advise you to do not one damn thing."

Confusion knitting her brow, Hadley said, "Say what?"

Folding her arms over her chest, Belinda doubled down. "You heard me. You didn't dime him out, so he's in the wrong here. So you need to stop calling and texting him, and go on about your business. When he realizes how stupid he's been, he'll be back."

"I don't know about that, B. He was pretty angry."

"Yep. And he'll be just as contrite when he comes to his damn senses." Belinda gave her a curt nod. "Trust me, girl."

"Despite your lack of a man?" Hadley knew her skepticism showed in her expression.

Belinda rolled her eyes. "Yes, because my lack of a man is by choice. It certainly isn't from a lack of offers." She flipped her ponytail and winked.

Snickering despite her mood, Hadley shook her head at her friend's shenanigans. "Girl, you're crazy."

"That may be so, but I'm right, too." She rested her back against the armrest, as if indicating that her job was done.

Viola headed for the kitchen. "Okay, enough of this depressing talk. I say we watch a movie, and I'll make the popcorn."

"Great idea." Belinda was already shrugging out of her jacket. "Don't you have *Beyond the Lights* on DVD?"

"Yeah." Knowing that neither of her houseguests

was leaving any time soon, Hadley got up and went to her entertainment center.

Her mother and her best friend were real pieces of work, and she felt fortunate to have them in her life.

Devon stood in his mother's kitchen Sunday morning, filling his plate with her famous breakfast. Though she'd lived in Los Angeles for more than a decade now, Eva Sykes Granger hadn't lost her touch for Southern cooking. As he loaded up with cheese-laden eggs, country sausage, seasoned grits and fluffy biscuits running with butter, he smiled for the first time in a few days.

As he carried his bounty to the table to join his parents, he took in the familiar room, the heart of his parents' home. He'd purchased the twenty-five-hundred-square-foot Echo Park home for them after the success of *Reach for the Sky*, his first Western film. And while his mother had initially complained about his "extravagant" gift, declaring the house "too large for folks our age," she'd soon forgotten her protests and started decorating. The kitchen was painted a dark blue and white, displaying a blueberry motif in honor of Eva's favorite fruit.

Sitting down, he grabbed the little ceramic bunch of blueberries that held the black pepper and sprinkled a bit onto his eggs.

Eva was already eating, her eyes on the pages of *Better Homes & Gardens*. Her white hair was up in curlers, and she wore a blue T-shirt and a pair of bedazzled blue windbreaker pants. In her hand was her favorite mug, emblazoned with the words *49 and Hold-*

*ing.* The cup held her favorite blend of herbal tea, since she didn't like coffee.

Across from her, David Granger flipped through that day's edition of the *LA Times*. He was bald, having long ago given up the ghost regarding his receding hairline. His thick eyebrows and trimmed mustache were the color of fresh-fallen snow, standing out in contrast to his deep skin tone. As he read, he absently nibbled on a biscuit, the crumbs falling onto his Marine Corps sweatshirt.

With a contented sigh, Devon dug into his breakfast. This was why he'd come here from the airport instead of going home. It would be several more weeks before he could stand in one spot long enough to cook, so his mother's cuisine had drawn him. But beyond that, he felt a certain peace in the presence of his parents. They were about as laid-back as parents could be.

Devon was chewing a forkful of eggs when he heard his father clear his throat.

"Now, Eva?" David asked the question without looking up from the local section of his newspaper.

She glanced up from her magazine, looking right at her son. "Yes, David. Now is good."

A confused Devon looked back and forth between his parents while tucking a piece of sausage between the split halves of his biscuit. "What's up?"

This time David closed his paper and folded it up. Resting his arms on the tabletop, he tented his fingers.

*Uh-oh.* Devon's eyes widened. Nothing good ever came of his father's finger tenting, at least not where he was concerned. He felt like a wayward teen, staring down the business end of an epic lecture.

David cleared his throat again. "What's going on with you, son?"

He blinked a few times. "Um, nothing."

David scoffed. "Something brought you here. And you may as well tell us what it is."

"You know we love having you, baby," Eva added. "And you're welcome to come and stay with us anytime. But we're entitled to know what's going on with you."

Feeling out of sorts, he shrugged. "I'm not supposed to be cooking, remember? And where else am I gonna get real Southern food cooked with this much love?" He hoped flattery would distract his mother from this rare quest to find out about his personal life.

It didn't. "Nice try, Devon. But I brought you into this world, and I know something's on your mind." Eva sipped her tea. "So, spill it."

Taken aback, Devon dropped his fork and put his hands up. "Now, wait a minute. What makes y'all so sure there's something wrong?"

David fielded that question. "You've been moping around this house ever since you got back from the island. Don't think we haven't noticed."

"Not only that, but you're been eating everything I cook, as fast as I can make it," Eva quipped as she flipped the page in her magazine.

"Sure enough." David reached out and patted his son's belly. "Much more of your mama's cooking and you gonna pop, son." He winked. "Why don't you go on and tell us what the problem is."

It had become clear he couldn't squirrel his way out of this conversation, so Devon acquiesced. "Can I at least finish my breakfast first?"

"Go ahead." Eva nodded in his direction. "We'll wait."

Shaking his head, Devon scooped up the last of his grits and eggs, then tucked the last piece of biscuit in his mouth. As he ate, he wondered how to best phrase his "problem," though he considered it more of a revelation. Washing down the food with a long swig of orange juice, he set the glass down. "My holiday vacation was a little more eventful than I'd hoped."

"That's pretty obvious, from the way you've been acting." David took a draw from his mug of black coffee. "Can you be a little more specific?"

He sighed. "Y'all remember Hadley Monroe, right?"

Eva's face brightened at the mention of her name. "I sure do remember little Hadley. Those rambunctious brothers of hers kept her running all the time when you all were younger. How is she doing?"

Devon slanted his eyes in his mother's direction. "First, she's not so little anymore. She's twenty-eight. And…she and I started dating while I was in Sapphire Shores."

David grinned, slapping his open palm on the table. "Well, hot damn. Never would have thought of you two as a match."

"She's a real sweet girl, so you've got my approval." Eva closed her magazine. "But I know that's not why you're sitting around my house looking like a little lost puppy."

He gave his mother a wry smile. "Actually, it is. Hadley and I already broke up."

David's brow crinkled. "Well, that was short-lived, then."

"Yeah, it was." *And it's a damn shame.* "For a while there, I thought she was the one."

Eva exchanged a look with her husband. "And what changed that?"

"She showed me who she really is." Draining the last of his orange juice, Devon stood and took his dishes to the sink. "She can't be trusted."

Quiet settled over the room for a moment, making the sound of the china dishes landing in the stainless-steel sink seem much louder. Walking back to the table, he sat down.

Both of his parents eyed him expectantly—waiting for him to elaborate, he assumed. So he told them about the night at Oceanview Grill when the paparazzi had shown up, seemingly out of nowhere. "In all the years I've been vacationing back home, this has never happened before."

Eva frowned. "How does that make it Hadley's fault?"

"I wouldn't even have considered that angle, Mama, until one of the photographers looked right at Hadley and called her by name. Asked her why she'd tipped them off if she didn't want to be photographed." He scoffed. "I guess he was surprised that we went out of our way to avoid him and his ilk."

David shook his head. "Did you ever ask her if she contacted them, Devon?"

He thought about it for a moment. As he recalled, he hadn't so much asked her as he had accused her. "I asked her why she did it."

Rolling his eyes, David got up from the table. "Eva, you take this one. This boy is obviously out of his mind." Tucking his folded newspaper under his arm, he shuffled out of the room.

Eva fixed her son with a hard glare. "I know you're not going to sit here at my table and tell me you accused that girl of betraying you without even giving her a chance to tell her side."

Singed by his mother's fiery gaze, he looked away. "Mama, all she had to say was that she didn't do it. She never even admitted—"

"Hush up." She sat her mug down. "Son, you ought to be ashamed of yourself. I've never known Hadley to be dishonest, have you?"

Unable to think of such an occasion, he shook his head.

"I can't believe you. You were probably so busy yelling at her that you missed the whole point of what she was telling you." Folding her arms over her chest, she continued. "Have you even considered that she's telling the truth? That she wasn't the one who called those people?"

Inhaling deeply, he realized his mother was right, as usual. He hadn't stopped to think about how vehemently Hadley had denied having a part in this debacle. "How did they get her name, then?"

Eva shrugged. "I don't know. That's for you to investigate if you want. But I tell you what." She stood, gathering her dishes and her husband's. "You're not going to sit in my house with your face all screwed up. You messed up, now do something about it." With a huff, she walked away with the armload of china and silverware.

Devon sat at the table alone for a few minutes, thinking over what had just happened. If his parents had noticed his foul mood and been concerned enough to bring it up—in direct contrast to how they usually operated—that meant something. It was quite a wake-up call.

He'd been missing Hadley fiercely—her smile, her touch, the sound of her voice. Even his anger did little to temper his longing for her. Taking his phone out, he dialed Mimi. He had arrangements to make.

*Mama's right. It's time to fix this.*

# Chapter 19

As Hadley looked through the papers she'd brought, she realized how unusually quiet the interior of Della's was. It was Monday, just after two. The morning New Year's Eve service crowd had already hit the deli, seeking to fill their grumbling stomachs after sitting through the sermon. She surmised that some of the other folks who usually stopped in had kicked off their New Year's celebrations early.

She sipped her iced tea, observing the gray day outside before returning her attention to her papers. One sheet among the stack was much larger than the others and occupied most of the square table, which was meant to seat four people. She'd taken it over when she came in, since no one had been sitting there, and she needed the space.

Della appeared behind the counter then. The older woman saw Hadley, waved and took a moment to slip her checked apron up over her head. Hanging the apron on a wall hook, she used a few pumps of hand sanitizer and made her way over to the table.

"Hi, Della. You ready?"

Sitting down, she grinned and clapped her hands together. "I sure am. I'm so excited about this."

Hadley returned the smile, looked around a bit. "Is Ralph going to sit in on this?"

Della shook her head. "You know how he is. He told me to look things over and decide, since this is my place."

"Okay, then." She spread out the large sheet. "I'm not an artist, but I brought over this diagram of MHI's last land plot. As you can see, I drew out the basic shape and location right here." She gestured to the rectangular object she'd added to the diagram with the tip of her pencil. "I think it's the perfect spot for the new Della's."

Eyes wide, Della looked over the image. "Are these dimensions in square feet?"

Hadley nodded.

"Wow. This is really a big building you're talking about." Della inhaled. "A big undertaking, too."

"I know. But you do good business here. Everybody agrees you're the best deli in town, way better than those two chain places." She tapped the rectangle for emphasis. "Having a space like this means you'll be able to accommodate everybody who wants to get into your place during the lunch rush."

Della sat back in her chair, as if thinking it over. "I

can see the benefit of that. Let me see what else you brought."

"Glad you asked." Opening a manila folder, Hadley pulled out the cost estimates and timelines. "I've got a friend who's an architect and another who's a contractor. Benefits of working in real estate. Here are the numbers they mocked up for you." She slid the small stack of papers across the table.

"There's a lot of information here."

"I know. Take your time going over it." Hadley got up and crossed the dining area with her frosted glass in hand. She stopped by the dispenser to refill her iced tea, then started back toward the table.

The bell over the entrance rang as the door swung open.

Hadley turned toward the sound and saw Savion standing there. She was still a little annoyed at the way he'd acted with Devon, but she supposed it didn't matter much now. "Hey, Savion."

"Hey, sis." He walked farther into the deli as she passed him, returning to the table with Della. Watching them, he asked, "Can a brother get some service?"

Della chuckled, "Boy, if you don't go on to the counter and order. Don't you see Marcelle standing there?" She gestured to the counter, where the young woman at the sandwich station waved.

"Okay, but I'll be back after I order." He went to the counter.

Della turned to Hadley. "That brother of yours is something else."

She rolled her eyes. "Trust me, I know."

"Handsome as all get-out, though." Della looked his way as she made the remark. "When the right woman comes along to tame him, he'll make a fine husband."

"Well, let's both pray for the day when that woman comes and takes him off my hands." Hadley giggled at the thought of her staid older brother strung out over this nameless, faceless woman. It was almost too much to hope for, but she had to admit she'd love to meet the lady who could capture his heart.

They chatted until Savion interrupted them, taking a seat at the next table with his sandwich and chips.

Sipping his drink, he asked, "What are you two doing?"

Hadley answered the question. "Well, Della is considering ways to expand her business. As for me, I'm taking the sage advice of my best friend by getting on with my life." She didn't want to think about Devon, so she pushed the thoughts away.

"You miss him, don't you?" Savion's eyes held hers, and he looked almost sympathetic.

"I thought you'd be happy about it." The words came out a bit snippier than she'd intended, but she couldn't take them back once she'd said them.

Savion didn't respond to that. Instead, he ate some of his food. He was quiet for so long, Hadley thought he was done talking. She returned her attention to the contracting estimates she'd had drawn up for Della.

Finally, he spoke again. "Hadley, I have something to tell you."

"What is it?" She glanced up from the estimates.

A deep sigh preceded his words. "I'm the one...who reached out to those photographers about Devon."

Hadley's eyes widened, her jaw tightening in anger. When she thought of what she'd lost because of her brother's actions... "Savion. How could you?"

He wore a mask of regret, and it looked genuine. "I'm sorry, Hadley. I used your work email to contact them—you had left your computer on."

She stood up, fists clenched at her sides. "I should pop you right upside your square head! I can't believe you."

"I know. It was childish and petty, and I really do regret it. I never expected things to blow up the way they did, but that doesn't matter." He pushed aside his half-eaten food. "I'd decided I didn't like Devon, that he wasn't good enough for you. I let the overprotective brother in me take over and did something against my better judgment."

"You're damn straight." She sat down again, flexing her fingers before the stiffness set in.

"Seeing you unhappy is driving me crazy. I had to confess, and I hope you'll forgive me. I promise I'll never pull a stunt like this again."

Della shook her head. "Honestly, Savion. I expect better of you."

He sighed. "I know. And from now on, better is what you'll get."

Hadley took several deep breaths. While she was angry with her brother, she also felt vindicated. This revelation solved the mystery of who'd ratted Devon out. Now that she knew, she felt better. But Devon...

"Savion, I'll forgive you under one condition."

"Anything. Just name it." He seemed contrite, and eager to get back in her good graces.

"Reach out to Devon and tell him what you just told me." She folded her arms over her chest. "This idea that I called in those photographers is what ruined things for us, so he needs to hear from the real culprit."

Savion nodded. "That's reasonable. I'll get in touch with him right away." He paused, as if he'd just thought of something. "But I can't guarantee this will fix things between you two."

"I'm not asking you to do that." She wasn't naive enough to think her brother had that ability. "Just tell him the truth. What he decides to do next is on him."

"Then I'm on it." He stood, tossing away his trash. "Is it too much to ask for a hug? Just so I know we're cool and you're not going to draw on my face while I'm asleep?"

She stood and hugged her brother, laughing at his reference to a prank she'd pulled on him when they were kids. "We're cool, if you do what I've asked. Screw this up, though, and you'll wake up looking like a Picasso."

The siblings separated, and Savion left.

After he was gone, Della asked, "What do you think is going to happen next?"

Hadley shrugged. "Who knows? I'm just going to wait and see."

"And keep living in the meantime."

Hadley smiled. "Yes, ma'am."

* * *

Devon rolled his bag across the polished floor of the concourse, moving at an easy pace. Spotting an empty seat in the terminal his connection would depart from, he strolled over and sat down. Jogging through airports was probably one of his least favorite ways to spend his time. But if the cause was worth it, he'd travel wherever it required.

He still had a good hour or so before his connecting flight, so he pulled out his tablet. He started putting together a virtual jigsaw puzzle to pass the time, but quickly lost interest in that. Turning off the tablet, he tucked it back into the outer pocket of his carry-on.

Absently watching the teeming crowd of people moving through the terminal, he couldn't keep his thoughts off Hadley. Did she miss him? Was she even thinking about him? He'd been so harsh with her the night he'd left the island. In his mind's eye, he could see her beautiful face, lined with worry as she tried to get through to him; he could see the tears coursing down her satin cheeks.

He'd hurt her, and he was having a hard time forgiving himself for that. She was about as sweet a woman as he'd ever encountered. Beneath the confidence she exuded lay sensitivity, and she'd made herself vulnerable by telling him how she felt about him. He'd repaid her bravery in revealing her innermost thoughts by basically calling her a liar and dismissing her attempts to explain herself.

He cursed under his breath, mentally kicking himself for being such an ass. Unfortunately, there was no way to go back and undo it now. All he could do was return to the island, and to her, and beg her forgiveness. He'd do whatever was necessary to prove that he loved her, tell her that he was sorry and that his life would be empty without her. He'd have to humble himself, let her inside to see the core of his being. He'd give her what he sensed she craved most: he'd trust her fully, the way she trusted him.

He'd been sitting there strategizing for about twenty minutes when his cell phone rang. Fishing it out of the hip pocket of his slacks, he answered it. "Hello?"

"Devon? It's Savion Monroe."

Surprise made him lean forward in his seat. "Hi, Savion."

"You sound surprised to hear from me."

"I am. I can't think of any reason you'd be calling me." And he couldn't. Despite the caffeine buzz from the two cups of coffee he'd had before leaving LAX, he couldn't think of a single motivation Savion would have for wanting to talk to him.

"I'll get right to it, then. I have something to tell you, related to my sister."

He rolled his eyes. "If this is about us seeing each other, I don't want to hear it."

Savion cleared his throat. "No, no. Nothing like that. I just want to clear up something about this whole paparazzi thing."

He shifted, seeking comfort on the chair's hard seat. *This ought to be interesting.* "And what's that?"

"I'm the one who tipped them off."

Devon frowned but said nothing. If Savion was feeling guilty enough to confess, he wanted to hear the whole story.

"Hadley has this bad habit of leaving her computer on at work, logged in to everything. So I used her email address to reach out to them."

He groaned. "You wanna tell me when you did this?"

"Christmas Eve. Took them a few days to get their crew together and make it to town, though. Then it was just a matter of figuring out where you would be." Savion paused. "I'm sorry, man. I really didn't expect things to turn out like this."

He was pretty sure Savion hadn't spent much time at all thinking about how things might turn out. It seemed the brother had mostly been concerned with driving a wedge between his sister and her new man. "I gotta say, man, this was a pretty childish stunt to pull. What are you, fourteen?"

Savion released a sigh. "I deserve that. I thought I was protecting my sister. The truth is, what I did was wrong. I shouldn't have interfered with her relationship, and it won't happen again."

"Did you tell Hadley what you did?"

"Yes. And she insisted I let you know, though I intended to do that anyway." Savion paused again, as if choosing his next words carefully.

Devon thought that wise.

"Look, she misses you. She's probably not going to call you, but if you do reach out to her, I know she'd be receptive."

Devon chuckled. "Oh, so you like me now?"

"In a word, yes. You make my sister happy, and that's all I ever really wanted for her."

He took a moment to let that settle in. Hearing Savion say those words made Devon feel good, maybe even a bit smug and self-righteous. But he was mature enough not to say any of that aloud.

"Would you consider giving her a call, Devon?"

He snorted a laugh. "I'll do you one better. I'm coming back for her."

Savion's tone brightened. "Really? When?"

Looking around the terminal, he smiled. "Actually, I'm at Chicago O'Hare right now. Should be there before nightfall, if all goes well."

"Awesome." Savion sounded genuinely pleased. "Listen, Devon, again, I'm sorry about all this."

"It's water under the bridge. As long as she's willing to take me back, I don't have any beef with you, Savion."

"Thanks, man. I appreciate it."

"Yeah. I respect your ability to admit to me that you acted like an idiot." He laughed. "Just don't do it again, and we're cool."

Savion laughed in response to that. "Trust me, my days of butting in on Hadley's life are over. Listen, when you get in town and have some time, call me. I'll take you out for a beer."

"Bet. Later, Savion." He disconnected the call, tucking his phone away. Sitting there in the terminal, he thought back on his mother's stern lecture. She'd been right about everything—Hadley had been telling the truth, but he'd been too blinded by his anger to see that.

It had been a long time since he'd been this wrong, and he was almost certain he'd have some tall apologizing to do when he arrived—if she would even talk to him.

It didn't matter, though. Being without her had taught him how much he needed her in his life. He needed her softness, her sweetness and, yes, even her sass. If she took him back, she could give him lip every day for the rest of his life if she wanted to, and he'd gladly accept it. She was the key to his future happiness, the only woman who'd managed to work her way into his heart since he'd become a widower.

Yes, Hadley Monroe was meant to be Mrs. Granger.

Now he just needed to get back to Sapphire Shores and prove it to her.

# Chapter 20

As day turned into night, Hadley settled in on her couch for a marathon of Eddie Murphy movies. Belinda had pestered her most of the day about going out to participate in the revelry of the night and bring in the New Year with some drinks and shenanigans. Hadley had turned her down, choosing a quiet night at home instead. The *Beverly Hills Cop* movies, *Coming to America* and *48 Hrs.* were on tap and sure to lift her mood. Besides, the New Year would come anyway, so she'd decided to spend the night in the comfort of her home rather than being pushed around some smoky club.

She started *Coming to America*, humming along with the iconic chant in the opening sequence as she fetched her popcorn and wine from the kitchen. Sitting down on the sofa, she placed the bowl in her lap.

During the scene where Prince Akeem and Semmi were deciding where to look for a suitable bride, a knock sounded at her door. She shook her head as she set her popcorn aside and climbed to her feet. *It's probably Belinda, trying to convince me to go out.* Her friend was about to be out of luck, because she'd removed her bra already and donned a rather matronly nightgown. Hadley wasn't going anywhere and no amount of convincing would change her mind.

Since it was dark outside, she stood on the tips of her toes to check the peephole as a precaution. Her brothers often lectured her about that.

When she saw Devon standing on the doorstep, her heart stopped. She dropped back down, wondering if she were seeing things. There was only one way to find out.

Opening the door, she saw that he really was standing there. Not only that, but he had another armful of roses—this time they were sterling. "Hi, baby."

Standing there in wide-eyed amazement, she managed to mutter a greeting. She let her hungry eyes devour his tall, handsome frame, draped in a pair of charcoal-gray slacks and a crisp white button-down shirt.

"These are for you." He handed her the flowers. "Mind if I come in?"

She took the roses, cradling them against her chest. Looking down at her nightgown, she sighed. "Here you are, looking like a million dollars, and I'm dressed like this."

He smiled. "You look beautiful to me."

She stepped back. "Come on in out of the cold."

Once he was inside and she shut and locked the door, he leaned against it. "Thank you for letting me in. After the way I treated you, I'm not sure I deserve your courtesy."

She blinked a few times. "I can't believe you're really here."

He reached out, dragging his fingertip over her jawline. "I'm here, baby. For real."

The tingle that went through her confirmed his words. Thinking of the flowers she still clutched, she took them to the kitchen. "Let me put these in water."

Once she'd taken care of the roses, she returned to the living room, where Devon remained in the same place, leaning against the door. He seemed to be waiting for her to say something. "Come over to the sofa and sit down."

Seated next to him, with the popcorn between them, she watched him, waiting.

He took a deep breath. "I'm sorry, Hadley. So very, very sorry."

She wanted to make him work for this, she really did. But the reality was that she'd missed him terribly. Hearing him apologize made happy tears spring to her eyes.

"Your brother called me today and admitted what he did. But even if he hadn't called, I was still wrong for the way I treated you, for not believing you."

Their gazes met.

"How did you get here so fast?"

He smiled. "Easy. I was already on my way—I was sitting in the terminal at O'Hare when he called."

She sniffled then as the tears continued to spill. Confusion mixed with her joy at seeing him again. "You were?"

"Yes." He moved the popcorn bowl, setting it on the coffee table. Before he moved, he asked, "Do you mind?"

She shook her head to let him know it was all right.

He scooted next to her, and his first move when he entered her personal space was to brush away her tears with the gentle touch of his fingertips. "I was on my way back already because I missed you. I realized how much I need you in my life, Hadley."

"I missed you, too." She could hear the emotion in her own voice, so she assumed he could hear it, as well.

He laid his hand against her cheek. "Again, I'm sorry, baby. Please forgive me. Regardless of what happened, I should have believed you. I should have trusted you."

She sobbed then, overwhelmed by the rising emotions of the moment.

"Please, don't cry. You've shown me what it means to truly trust someone." He tilted her face up, looked into her eyes. "And I trust you now. Completely and without reservation."

He kissed her then, and she welcomed it. Her lips parted immediately, allowing his tongue to search the depths of her mouth as she explored his. By the time she broke the kiss to catch her breath, she was panting as if she'd just run a fifty-yard dash.

He reached into his hip pocket and pulled out a small black velvet box.

She recognized the size and shape of it right away, and her hand flew to her mouth.

"I know this may seem sudden," he began as he rocked the lid open on its hinge. Inside was a cushion-cut sparkler on a rose-gold band. "But since you waited so long to tell me how you felt, I don't want to waste any more time. Hadley Aria Monroe, will you be my wife?"

"Yes!" She nodded, sticking her hand out for the ring. He slipped it on to her finger, and she admired its immense beauty. "This is gorgeous, Devon. How did you know that I like rose gold, and that my middle name is Aria?"

He shrugged. "Your brothers gave me all the information I needed."

She sighed happily, holding her hand up and turning it from side to side. She just loved the way it sparkled. "Seems those two knuckleheads are good for something. Guess I'll keep 'em."

He pulled her into his arms then, letting his desire show through in his gaze. "Fancy a little celebration, baby?"

She smiled a wicked smile. "Oh, hell yes. What better way to bring in the New Year than making love with my husband-to-be?"

He whistled. "See, that's why I love you. Beautiful, intelligent and freaky."

"Only when it comes to you." She leaned up for his kiss.

The kiss deepened, escalating into more, as passion rose between them. She straddled his lap, splaying her fingers across the back of his head as he brushed his lips over the tops of her breasts where the gown revealed them. She popped the buttons off his shirt in her eagerness to get him out of it, but neither of them cared.

Shirtless and breathing heavily, he stood, holding her close to him. She locked her legs around his waist, peppering his face and neck with kisses and licks. He felt a twinge in his back, but it was slight. It might mean taking an extra dose of his meds tomorrow. He moved across the room to the bare wall in the hallway, his big hands cupping her ass to support her body weight. In the hall, he pressed her back against the wall. He used one hand to rip open the snaps running down the front of her gown, and moments later, he drew her nipple into his warm mouth.

She sank her nails into his shoulders, her head coming to rest against the wall as the ecstasy built. They'd made love before, but nothing compared to this primal, passion-fueled encounter.

When he lifted his head from her breasts, he asked huskily, "Can I…"

She knew what he was asking, and she wanted it just as badly as he did. "Yes, Devon. Yes…" To further encourage him, she reached between them to undo the button and zipper on his trousers. Working them down around his powerful thighs, she groaned when he rubbed his hardness against her.

A few quick movements later, he'd freed his erection from his silk boxers. His searching fingers slid her panties aside, finding her center. She was hot with desire, and as he teased her a bit with his fingertips, her passion only grew.

"Now." She ground the word out through clenched teeth, pressing her pelvis against his.

He obliged her, pressing his length between her thighs and entering her in one swift, smooth motion.

A high-pitched cry left her throat as she experienced the sheer joy of him filling her.

And there, with the moonlight streaming in between the slats of the shutters, he made love to her until she screamed his name in the darkness.

Devon looked up at the cloudless blue sky, thankful for the warmth and beauty of the day. He stood on the beach, flanked by Campbell and Savion. They each wore crisp white shirts and black slacks, though Devon was the only one with a sterling rose pinned to his shirt pocket.

Belinda stood close by as well, wearing a lavender robe. She'd recently gotten ordained on the internet, at Hadley's request. Belinda wasn't especially religious, but if her outfit was any indication, she was taking her role as minister seriously—at least for the day.

From where they stood, they had a full view of the back of Monroe Manor and its grassy lawn, which was miraculously green despite the lingering winter.

That wasn't the view that concerned him, though. He was watching the back door, waiting for Hadley to make her appearance. He supposed he should be more patient, because it was a bride's prerogative to take her time getting ready on her special day. It seemed their relationship had spoiled him, because he'd gotten used to things flowing quickly but naturally between them.

It was early February, barely a month since he'd proposed, and they were already about to take their vows.

The old saying said, "You can't hurry love." As far as Devon was concerned, there wasn't any need. It moved fast enough without any interference from him.

Finally, she walked out on her father's arm. The white runner than had been spread out from the back door to the spot on the beach where everyone had gathered served as her path as she walked slowly toward him. He couldn't hold back his grin as he took in the sight of his radiant bride. She wore a white halter-top pantsuit encrusted with crystals and pearls. A sheer white coat covered her bare arms, and her feet were bare, save for the jewelry around her ankles. As he'd asked, she left her hair down, accenting her flowing curls with a large white flower tucked behind her ear.

By the time Carver placed his daughter's hand in her fiancé's, Devon could barely contain his excitement. He couldn't believe how incredibly fortunate he was. The fact that she'd agreed to be his wife seemed like a miracle to him.

They turned to Belinda, who performed the ceremony with a broad smile on her face the entire time. Devon was aware of the watchful gazes of their parents, her brothers and the few friends he'd invited, but he had eyes only for his bride. He spoke his vows loud and clear, to let her know that he had no doubts about their future. She spoke hers in kind, and the softness in her eyes as she pledged her love to him touched his heart.

When Belinda pronounced them man and wife, Hadley threw her hands in the air and gave a little cheer.

He cut her impromptu celebration short by pulling her into his arms for a lingering kiss.

The party went on late into the evening, underneath a tent the Monroes had set up in their backyard. Sitting in the throne-like chair he'd been assigned, Devon cradled his wife's hand in his own.

She stood suddenly, then leaned down to kiss him on the forehead. "I've gotta go to the little brides' room. I'll be right back."

After she walked away, Savion strolled up, a glass of champagne in his hand. He reached out to shake his brother-in-law's hand. "Welcome to the family, man."

"Thanks."

"Got a little something for you. Call it a wedding gift."

Devon leaned forward in his chair. "Aw, Savion. You didn't have to…"

"Listen up, Devon. Remember what you said a couple of weeks ago about opening a production studio here on the island?"

He nodded. "Of course. I've been looking into what I need to do, and I'm ready to make some moves as soon as I find a location."

Savion winked. "You're in luck. Neville South withdrew their proposal, so…it looks like that last piece of Monroe family property is yours now." He reached into his shirt pocket, pulled out a folded sheet of paper and passed it to him.

Opening it, Devon's eyes widened. "It's the deed to the land plot."

"Congrats, man." Savion turned and started to walk away.

"Hold up, Savion. This is too much. I mean, I can buy the land…"

Carver strode up then, smiling. "Nonsense. It's my wedding gift to you, and in our family, we don't turn down generous gifts such as this." He patted him on the shoulder. "Just say thank you, son."

An amazed Devon parroted his new father-in-law. "Thank you, son."

Chuckling, Savion and Carver walked away.

When Hadley returned, she climbed into his lap instead of returning to her own throne. "What's up? Your expression tells me I missed something."

He passed her the deed. "Looks like we have land for my studio."

She covered her mouth, tears springing to her eyes. "Wow."

"Come on, don't cry." He used his thumb to dash away her tears.

She looked into his eyes then. "Stay with me forever, and I won't have any reason to."

He touched her cheek. "It's a deal."

And to seal the arrangement, he pressed his lips to hers.

\* \* \* \* \*

# COMING NEXT MONTH
## Available December 19, 2017

### #553 PLAYING WITH SEDUCTION
*Pleasure Cove* • by Reese Ryan

Premier event promoter Wesley Adams is glad to be back in North Carolina. Until he discovers the collaborator on his next venture is competitive volleyball player Brianna "Bree" Evans, the beauty he spent an unforgettable evening with more than a year ago. Will their past cost them their second chance?

### #554 IT'S ALWAYS BEEN YOU
*The Jacksons of Ann Arbor* • by Elle Wright

Best friends Dr. Lovely "Love" Washington and Dr. Drake Jackson wake up in a Vegas hotel to discover not only did they become overnight lovers, they're married. But neither remembers tying the knot. Will they finally realize what's been in front of them all along—true love?

### #555 OVERTIME FOR LOVE
*Scoring for Love* • by Synithia Williams

Between school, two jobs and caring for her nephew, Angela Bouler is keeping it all together...until Isaiah Reynolds bounces into her life. Angela's hectic life doesn't quite mesh with the basketball star's image of the perfect partner. Winning her heart won't be easy, but it's the only play that matters...

### #556 SOARING ON LOVE
*The Cardinal House* • by Joy Avery

Tressa Washington will do anything to escape the disastrous aftermath of her engagement party. Even stow away in the back of Roth Lexington's car and drive off with the aerospace engineer. In his snowbound cabin, they'll learn that to reach the heights of love, they'll have to be willing to fall...

KPCNM1217

# Get 2 Free Books,
## Plus 2 Free Gifts—
### just for trying the
### Reader Service!

KIMANI™ ROMANCE

*LOVE*
# Harlequin romance?

Join our Harlequin community to share your thoughts and connect with other romance readers!

Be the first to find out about promotions, news, and exclusive content!

Sign up for the Harlequin e-newsletter and download a free book from any series at

**www.TryHarlequin.com**

---

**CONNECT WITH US AT:**

Harlequin.com/Community

 Facebook.com/HarlequinBooks

Twitter.com/HarlequinBooks

 Instagram.com/HarlequinBooks

Pinterest.com/HarlequinBooks

ReaderService.com

 **HARLEQUIN**®

**ROMANCE WHEN
YOU NEED IT**

HSOCIAL2017

Need an adrenaline rush from nail-biting tales
(and irresistible males)?

Check out **Harlequin® Intrigue®**
and **Harlequin® Romantic Suspense** books!

## New books available every month!

---

## CONNECT WITH US AT:

Harlequin.com/Community

 Facebook.com/HarlequinBooks

Twitter.com/HarlequinBooks

Instagram.com/HarlequinBooks

Pinterest.com/HarlequinBooks

ReaderService.com

**ROMANCE WHEN
YOU NEED IT**

SGENRE2017